Erin felt that same prickle of awareness as when their hands had touched over the scones. But this time, instead of avoiding eye contact, she looked him straight in the eye. Nate's pupils were dilated to the point where his eyes looked almost black.

Oh, help. It looked as if this attraction she felt towards him was mutual, then. What were they going to do about it? Because this situation was impossible.

His face was serious. 'Erin.' He reached out and cupped her cheek in his palm, then brushed his thumb over her lower lip.

She felt hot all over and her skin tingled where he touched her.

'Nate. We're right in the middle of the hospital,' she whispered.

'And anyone could see us. I know.' He moved his hand away. 'Erin, I think we need to talk.'

She knew he was right. 'But not here.' It was too public.

'Where? When?' His voice was urgent.

'You said Caitlin would be all right with your mum for a while.' She took a deep breath. Maybe she needed to be brave about this, as Mikey had suggested. Do it now. Tell him the truth. And if he walked away—well, it just proved that she'd been stupid to let him matter to her. 'My place, right now?'

Dear Reader,

I'd got to that stage of life where I'm really fascinated by gardens—and then my friend Michelle told me about a news story of a sensory garden for spinal patients. What a perfect setting, I thought. Especially when I kept seeing stories about spinal patients in the news.

But who would get involved with a sensory garden? And who would think it was a bad idea?

Meet Erin, who has a lot of shadows in her past, and Nate, who has a lot of shadows in his present.

The sensory garden starts by keeping them apart, and then it is very instrumental in bringing them together. Add in a troubled teen—who reminds Erin very much of herself at that age—complicated families and the whole idea about how love happens when you least expect it…and you have what happens with Erin and Nate.

I hope you enjoy their journey—and that the garden inspires you as much as it did me.

I'm always delighted to hear from readers, so do come and visit me at katehardy.com.

With love,

Kate Hardy

CAPTURING THE SINGLE DAD'S HEART

BY
KATE HARDY

First published in Great Britain 2016
By Mills & Boon, an imprint of HarperCollins*Publishers*
1 London Bridge Street, London, SE1 9GF

Large Print edition 2017

© 2016 Pamela Brooks

ISBN: 978-0-263-06675-3

Our policy is to use papers that are natural, renewable
and recyclable products and made from wood grown
in sustainable forests. The logging and manufacturing
processes conform to the legal environmental
regulations of the country of origin.

Printed and bound in Great Britain
by CPI Antony Rowe, Chippenham, Wiltshire

Kate Hardy always loved books, and could read before she went to school. She discovered Mills & Boon books when she was twelve and decided this was what she wanted to do. When she isn't writing Kate enjoys reading, cinema, ballroom dancing and the gym. You can contact her via her website: katehardy.com.

Books by Kate Hardy

Mills & Boon Medical Romance

Dr Cinderella's Midnight Fling
Once a Playboy…
The Brooding Doc's Redemption
A Date with the Ice Princess
Her Real Family Christmas
200 Harley Street: The Soldier Prince
It Started with No Strings…
A Baby to Heal Their Hearts
A Promise…to a Proposal?
Her Playboy's Proposal

Mills & Boon Cherish

A New Year Marriage Proposal
It Started at a Wedding…
Falling for Mr December
Billionaire, Boss…Bridegroom?
Holiday with the Best Man

Visit the Author Profile page at millsandboon.co.uk for more titles.

To Michelle Styles,
with love and thanks for the lightbulb

CHAPTER ONE

WHY WOULD YOU turn down every single invitation to a team night out when you were new to the department? Erin wondered. Surely you'd want to get to know your colleagues and help yourself fit in to the team more quickly, rather than keep your distance?

Nate Townsend was a puzzle.

As a colleague, he was fine; she'd done a few ward rounds with him, and had been pleased to discover that he was good with their patients. He listened to their worries, reassured them and explained anything they didn't understand without showing the least bit of impatience. The team in Theatre had all been thrilled to report that, unlike the surgeon he'd replaced, Nate was precise with his instructions and always bothered to thank the nursing staff.

But he didn't socialise with the team at all.

There was always a polite but guarded smile, a rueful shrug of the shoulders, and, 'Sorry, I can't make it,' when anyone asked him to join them. No excuses, no explanations. Just a flat no: whether it was a drink, a meal, going ten-pin bowling or simply catching the latest movie. He didn't even have lunch or coffee with any of his colleagues in the spinal unit; he grabbed a sandwich at his desk instead and wrote up his notes so he could leave straight at the end of his shift.

Erin knew that some people preferred to keep themselves to themselves, but she'd been working at the London Victoria since her first year as a junior doctor, and the friendliness of her colleagues had always made even the most harrowing day more bearable. Why did Nate rebuff everyone? Did he have some kind of complicated home life that meant he needed to be there as much as he could outside work and just didn't have the energy to make friends with his colleagues?

Not that it was any of her business.

Then she became aware that Nick, the head of their department, was talking to her.

She really ought to be paying attention in the

monthly staff meeting instead of puzzling over her new colleague.

And it wasn't as if she was interested in Nate anyway, even if it turned out that he was single. Erin was very firmly focused on her career. She'd let her life be seriously derailed by a relationship when she was younger, and she was never going to make that mistake again. Friendship was all she'd ever offer anyone from now on. 'Sorry, Nick. I didn't quite catch that,' she said with a guilty smile.

'No problems. Can you bring us up to date on the sensory garden?'

Erin's pet project. The one that would help her make a real difference to their patients' lives. She smiled and opened her file. 'I'm pleased to report that we're pretty much ready to start. The hospital's agreed to let us transform the piece of land we asked for, the Friends of the London Victoria are working out a rota for the volunteers, and Ed's finalised the design—the committee just has to approve it. But they liked the draft version so it's pretty much a formality and we're planning to start the ground work in the next week or so.'

'Hang on,' Nate said. 'What's the sensory garden?'

'We're remodelling part of the hospital's grounds as a sensory garden, and making sure it's accessible to our patients,' Erin explained.

He frowned. 'That kind of project costs an awful lot of money. Wouldn't those funds be better spent on new equipment for the patients?'

This was Nate's first monthly team meeting, so he wouldn't know that Erin had been working on the garden project for almost a year in her spare time. She was sure he didn't mean to be rude, so she'd cut him some slack. 'I know that sensory gardens have a reputation for costing an arm and a leg, but this one's not going to cost anywhere near what you imagine,' she said with a smile. 'We already have the grounds, and the designer's working with us for nothing.'

'For nothing?' Nate looked sceptical.

'For publicity, then,' she said. 'The main thing is that he's not charging us for the actual design.' Like Erin herself, Ed the garden designer had a vested interest in the project. This was his way of giving something back, because the spinal unit at the London Victoria had treated his younger brother after a motorcycle accident. But it wasn't her place to tell Nate about their former patient. 'Actually, I hope he gets a ton of clients who respond to his generosity.'

'Hmm.' Nate's blue eyes were so dark, they were almost black. And right at that moment they were full of scepticism. Did he really have that bitter a view about human nature?

'The labour isn't costing us anything, either,' Erin continued. 'Ayesha—she's the chair of the Friends of the London Victoria—is setting up a rota of volunteers from across the community. So that's everyone from students who want some work experience for their CVs through to people who just enjoy pottering around in the garden in their spare time,' she explained. 'It's going to be a true community garden, so it will benefit everyone. And the rota's not just for planting the garden, it's for maintaining it as well.'

'What about the cost of the plants and any other materials used in the design?' Nate asked.

'Some things have been donated by local businesses,' she said, 'and the staff here, our patients and their families have been raising funds for the last year. We have enough money to cover the first phase of the project.'

'And you really think a sensory garden's the best way to spend that money?' he asked again.

Just who did the guy think he was? He'd been here almost a month, kept himself completely aloof from the team, and now he was criticising a project that had been months and months in the planning without having a single positive thing to say about it? Erin gritted her teeth in annoyance and, instead of letting her boss deal with it—the way she knew she should've done—she gave Nate Townsend her most acidic smile. If he wanted an answer, he'd get one.

'Actually, I do, and I'm not alone,' she said crisply. 'As you know, most of our patients have just had a massive and unexpected life change. They have to make a lot of adjustments—and they can be stuck inside in a clinical environment for months, just staring at the same four walls. A garden will be a restful space for them to sit in and have some quiet time with family and friends, chat with other patients, or even just sit and read in a space that's a bit different. It'll help them start getting used to their new lives rather than just feeling that they're stuck inside the same four walls all the time with no greenery. A sensory garden has scent, sound, texture, colour and even taste—all things that stimulate our patients and can help with their recovery.'

'You said a restful space,' Nate repeated. 'How are you going to find that in the centre of London, with traffic going past all the time?'

'Fair point,' she conceded, understanding his scepticism on that particular subject, 'but we're using hedging to lessen the impact of the traffic noise. You're very welcome to have a copy of the plans.' She looked him straight in the eye. 'Constructive comments from someone with relevant experience are always welcome.'

His eyes widened slightly to acknowledge the point of her comment; clearly he understood that she didn't think he was being constructive at all or had any relevant experience.

But that didn't stop him asking more questions. 'So what about the fact that some of our patients have problems regulating their temperature and can get either too hot or too cold in a garden?'

'Phase two,' she said, 'will be a covered space to help those particular patients. But we're beginning the first phase now so our patients and their families can start to benefit from the garden as soon as possible, rather than having to wait until we have all the money for the second phase. And, before you mention the fact that our patients are usually confined to wheelchairs, we're making sure that the pathways have no bumps and are smooth-running for anyone in a chair. Actually, Ed—the landscape designer—even spent a few hours being wheeled about the grounds in a chair so he could see for himself where the problems are.'

'Right.' But Nate still didn't look convinced.

She sighed. 'I did a lot of research before I suggested the project. And I've visited sensory gardens both in England and in Scandinavia.' The glint in his eye made her add, 'At my own cost, during my annual leave.'

'Very public-spirited of you,' he drawled.

She was really starting to dislike him now. How dared he judge her?

Though there was some truth in his barb. The

whole reason she'd thrown herself behind the sensory garden project was because she'd seen the difference it had made to her brother. And helping to make that same difference to their patients might go some way towards lessening her guilt about what had happened to Mikey.

Might. She knew that her brother had forgiven her a long time ago, but she still couldn't forgive herself.

'It's important,' she said quietly. 'From a medical point of view, exposure to nature helps with pain management, reduces stress and increases feelings of calm and relaxation.'

He shrugged. 'That's a bit New Agey, don't you think?'

'Apart from the fact that garden therapy has been used as far back as ancient Greece,' Erin pointed out, 'in modern terms you can actually measure the effect on the patient's blood pressure and heart rate. Plus a change of scene makes a mental difference. It might be a very small thing to you and me, and we all probably take it for granted, but for a patient who's been stuck inside for weeks it's a *massive* thing to be able to go outside.'

Finally, to Erin's relief, Nick spoke up. 'As the project's already been agreed, perhaps we should all just agree to disagree on the use of funds and what have you.'

'Sure,' Nate said easily. 'And, as the new boy, I know I shouldn't make waves. But my sister's a deputy headmistress, and she tells me that the thing she likes best about having a new governor on the team is that you get a critical friend—someone who looks at things from the outside with a fresh pair of eyes and asks questions. I guess I was trying to do the same thing here.'

'You're very welcome to a copy of the file,' Erin said again, 'if you want to check the costings and make sure I haven't missed anything.'

'I'll take you up on that,' he said.

Erin simmered through the rest of the meeting. Critical friend, indeed. There was nothing *friendly* about Nate Townsend. He might be easy on the eye—on his first day, several of her female colleagues had declared him one of the sexiest men they'd ever met, with his Celtic good looks of dark hair, pale complexion and navy blue eyes—but in her view character was much more important than looks. And she really didn't like what she'd seen of Nate Townsend today.

And of course she *would* have to do the ward rounds with him after the meeting.

'Do you have a particular way you'd prefer to do the ward rounds this morning?' she asked, knowing that she sounded snippy but not being able to stop herself.

'I'm quite happy to follow the normal protocol here,' he said mildly.

'That's not the impression you gave in the meeting.' The words were out before she could hold them back.

'I apologise if I upset you,' he said. 'Why is the garden so important to you?'

He seriously thought she was going to tell him that—so he could go ahead and judge her as harshly as she judged herself? No way. 'I've been working on the project for a year,' she said instead. 'And I've seen the difference it's made to patients elsewhere. Phase one is the garden, phase two is the covered area, and maybe we can have some raised beds in phase three and a greenhouse so the patients can grow plants. If it proves to them that they can still do something, that they can still contribute to life instead of having to be looked after every second of the day and feel like a burden to everyone, it'll help them adjust to their new life and the prospect of having to change their career.'

'I think Nick's right,' Nate said, his expression inscrutable. 'For now we'll agree to disagree.'

She inclined her head. 'As you wish. Though I'd be interested to know why you're so against the project.'

'Because several times before now I've seen funds raised to help patients and then wasted on people's pet hobbyhorses,' he said.

Deep breath, she told herself. He might be right about it being her pet hobbyhorse, but the rest of it was way off the mark. 'I can assure you that what we're doing isn't a waste of funds. And it's not just about the patients. As I said, it's a community garden, with local volunteers helping. That's everyone from older people who've moved into a flat and miss having a garden through to young mums who want just a couple of hours a week doing something that's not centred around the baby, and the local sixth form's involved, too. It's a project that gives extra credit towards exams for some of them, and others can talk about it on their personal statement when they apply to university. It's getting everyone working together to make a difference and absolutely everyone involved gets some benefit from it. I'm sorry if you see a garden as a waste of money, but the rest of us really don't.'

Erin was really passionate about this project, Nate thought. Her face had been full of animation when she'd talked about the garden and what she thought it could do for their patients.

Then he shook himself mentally. Yes, Erin Leyton was pretty, with her curly light brown hair caught back at the nape of her neck, clear grey eyes and a dusting of freckles across her nose. But, even if he were in a place where he could think about having a relationship—which he most definitely wasn't, with his life being in utter chaos right now—it would be way too complicated, given that they had such opposing views on fundamental things.

Though maybe he was only being scratchy with her because he was so frustrated with how things were going outside work, and that wasn't fair of him. It wasn't Erin's fault that his ex-wife had dropped a bombshell on him only a week before he'd started his new job and he'd been running round like a headless chicken ever since, trying to sort everything out. And it definitely wasn't Erin's fault that he hated himself for being such a failure.

'I'm sorry,' he said. 'You're right—it's like the new boy stamping everywhere to try and make an impression.'

'I didn't say that.'

'You were thinking it, though.'

She gave him a rueful smile. 'Can you blame me?'

'No—and actually, it isn't that at all. I apologise. I shouldn't bring my baggage to work.'

The hostility in her grey eyes melted in an instant. 'Apology accepted. And sometimes,' she said quietly, 'it helps to have someone to talk to—someone who isn't involved with the situation and won't judge you or spread gossip.'

She was offering him a shoulder to cry on, even after he'd been combative towards her in a meeting involving what was clearly her pet project? That was unbelievably generous. Then again, he wasn't that surprised. He'd already noticed Erin's name at the top of all the internal memos organising a team night out or a collection for someone's birthday or baby shower. He had a feeling that she was one of life's fixers.

Well, his life couldn't be fixed right now. He wasn't sure if it ever could be. 'Thanks for the offer,' he said, 'but I don't really know you.'

She shrugged, but he could see the momentary flash of hurt on her face. 'Fair enough. Forget I said anything.'

He felt like a heel, but he couldn't even offer anyone friendship at the moment. Not until he'd sorted things out with Caitlin and established a better relationship with her. And he had no idea how long that was going to take. Right now it felt like it was never going to happen.

'Let's do the ward rounds,' he said. 'We have

Kevin Bishop first. He's forty-five, but he has the spine of a sixty-five-year-old—it's a really bad case of stenosis.'

'Is that from normal wear and tear,' she asked, 'or is it job-related?'

'Probably a bit of both. He's a builder. He has two worn discs, and the sheath around his spinal cord has narrowed,' Nate explained.

'Which would put pressure on his spinal nerves—so it sounds as if the poor guy's been in a lot of pain,' she said, her face full of sympathy.

'He's been taking anti-inflammatories,' Nate said, 'but he says they don't even touch the pain any more.'

'So you're looking at major surgery and weeks of rehabilitation?' she asked. 'If so, Mr Bishop could be a candidate for the sensory garden.'

'No, no and no,' Nate said. 'He won't be here for long. I'm planning to use an interspinous spacer device this afternoon rather than doing a laminectomy.'

'I've read about that,' she said. 'Isn't there a larger risk of the patient needing to have surgery again in the future if you use a spacer rather than taking a slice of bone off the area putting pressure on his spinal cord?'

'Yes, but there's also a much lower risk of complications than you'd get from taking off the bit of bone that rubs and causes the pain, plus it's just a small incision and he'll be out again in a couple of days. I'd normally use the procedure for older patients or those with higher risks of surgery,' Nate said. 'Kevin Bishop is still young but, given that he's overweight and has high blood pressure, I think he's higher risk.'

'Fair enough. So how exactly does the spacer work?'

Nate could see that she was asking from a professional viewpoint rather than questioning his competence; he knew that Erin was a neurologist rather than a surgeon. 'We'll put a spacer into his lower vertebrae. It'll act as a supportive spring and relieve the pressure on the nerve. It gives much better pain relief than epidural steroid injections, plus the spinal nerves aren't exposed so there's a much lower risk of scarring.' He paused. Maybe this would be a way of easing the tension between them after that meeting.

'Provided Mr Bishop gives his consent, you can come and watch the op, if you like.'

'Seriously?' She looked surprised that he'd even offered.

'Seriously.' Was she going to throw it back in his face, or accept it as the offer of a truce?

'I'd really like that. Thank you.' She smiled at him.

Again Nate felt that weird pull of attraction and reminded himself that this really wasn't appropriate. For all he knew, Erin could be in a serious relationship. Not that he was going to ask, because he didn't want her to think that he was interested in her. He didn't have the headspace or the mental energy right now to be interested in anyone. His focus needed to be on his daughter and learning how to be a good full-time dad to her. 'Uh-huh,' he said, feeling slightly awkward, and went with Erin to see his patient.

He introduced her swiftly to Kevin Bishop.

'I've reviewed the scans of your spine, Mr Bishop, and your blood tests are all fine, too, so I'm happy to go ahead with surgery today,' he said. 'Would you mind if Dr Leyton here sits in on the operation?'

'No, that's fine,' Mr Bishop said, looking relieved. 'I'm just glad you're going to do it today. I'm really looking forward to being able to tie my own shoelaces again, and to stand up without my legs tingling all the time.'

'It's been that bad?' Erin asked sympathetically.

Mr Bishop nodded. 'The pain's been terrible. Rest doesn't help and the tablets don't seem to work any more. My doctor said I'd have to have surgery—I was dreading the idea of being stuck in hospital for weeks, but Mr Townsend said that I'd only be in for a few days.' He gave her a weary smile. 'I just want to be able to play football with my kids again and get back to my job.'

'The surgery will make things much better,' Nate promised. 'I know we talked about it before, but I'd like to run through the situation again to make sure you're happy about what's happening.'

Mr Bishop nodded.

'Basically what happens is that the nerves in your spine run down a tunnel called the spinal canal. You've had a lot of wear and tear on your spine, and that makes the spinal canal narrower; that means it squeezes the nerves when you stand or walk, which is why you're getting pain. What I want to do is put a spacer between two of the bones in your spine, and that will relieve the pressure and stop the pain. Now, you haven't eaten anything since last night?'

'No, though I'm dying for a cup of tea,' Mr Bishop admitted.

Nate smiled. 'Don't worry, you'll get your cup of tea this afternoon. I'll get the pre-op checks organised now and I'm going to operate on you at two. The operation's going to be under a local anaesthetic, but you'll also be sedated so you won't remember anything about it afterwards. You'll be lying face down during the operation on a special curved mattress; that will reduce the pressure on your chest and pelvis, and also give me better access to your spine.'

'How long will the operation take?' Mr Bishop asked.

'It should be about an hour or so, depending on what I find—but from your scan it looks pretty straightforward.'

'That's great.' Mr Bishop smiled. 'I still can't believe I'll be able to go home again in a couple of days. I thought I'd be stuck in here for weeks.'

'You're not going to be able to go straight back to work or to drive for the first few weeks after the operation,' Nate warned, 'and you'll need to do physiotherapy and exercises. They'll start about four weeks after the op—and in the meantime it'll be better for you to sit on a high, hard chair than a soft one with a low back.'

'And no bending or lifting?'

'Absolutely. Listen to whatever the physiotherapist tells you,' Nate said. 'This is a newish procedure, Mr Bishop. I do need to tell you that, because it's so new, there's a very small possibility the spacer might move in the future or need replacing.'

'If it takes the pain away, I can cope with that.'

Nate talked Mr Bishop through the likely complications and all the possible consequences of the operation, then asked him to sign the consent form. 'I'll see you later this afternoon,' he said with a smile.

* * *

Later that afternoon, watching Nate perform in Theatre, Erin was spellbound. His instructions to Theatre staff were clear, he was polite as well as precise and he talked her through every single step of the operation, explaining the methodology and what it would do for the patient.

With their patient and in Theatre, he was a completely different man, she thought. Not the cool, critical and judgemental stranger he'd been in the meeting. This man had deft, clever hands and really knew his stuff—and he treated everyone around him as his equal. She noticed that he made the time to thank every member of the team at the end of the operation, too.

This Nate Townsend, she thought, was a man she'd like to get to know.

And she understood now why so many of her colleagues had dubbed him the sexiest surgeon in the hospital. The only bit of his face she could see clearly was his eyes—a gorgeous, sensual dark blue. And the combination of intelligence and clever hands made a shiver of pure desire run down her spine.

Which was totally inappropriate.

She was here to observe, not to go off in some ridiculous, lust-filled daydream.

'Thank you for letting me observe, today,' she said when they'd both scrubbed out. 'That was really useful. I can talk to patients with spinal stenosis about their options with a lot more authority now.'

'No problem. And if you have any questions about the procedure later, come and find me.'

He actually smiled at her, then, and she caught her breath. When he smiled like that—a smile that came from inside, more than just politeness—he was utterly gorgeous.

And he was probably involved with someone. Given that he kept everyone at a distance, she'd bet that his home life was full of complications. And none of those complications were any of her business.

'See you tomorrow,' she said, feeling slightly flustered.

'Yeah.'

Once Nate was happy that Kevin Bishop and his other patients from Theatre that afternoon had settled back on the ward and there were no complications following surgery, he finished writing up his notes. And then he braced himself for the drive to his mother's house.

Guilt flooded through him. What kind of a father was he, to dread picking up his own daughter? But being her full-time parent—the one with total responsibility—was a far cry from being the part-time dad who saw her for a few snatched days in school holidays and odd weekends. Before Caitlin had come to live with him, they hadn't spent long enough together at a stretch to run out of things to talk about. Now, it was the other way round: he had all the time he could've wanted with her, and not a clue what to say.

As he'd half expected, Caitlin wasn't in the mood for talking.

'How was your day?' he asked as he pulled away from the kerb.

Her only answer was a shrug.

Great. What did he ask now? Clearly she didn't want to talk about school or her friends—he didn't even know whether she'd made friends, yet, because she always sidestepped the question whenever he asked.

Food would be a safe subject, surely? 'Do you fancy pizza for dinner tonight?'

A shake of her head. 'Your mother already cooked for me.'

As part of her protest about being forced to move from Devon to London, Caitlin had shut off from Sara, her paternal grandmother; she avoided calling Sara anything at all, just as she'd stopped calling Nate 'Dad'. He had no idea how to get round that without starting another row—and he was trying to pick his battles carefully.

By the time he'd thought of another topic, they were home. Not that Caitlin considered his house as her real home, and he was beginning to wonder if she ever would. Though neither of them had any choice in the matter.

'Do you have much homework?' he tried as he unlocked the front door.

'I've already done it. Do you have to be on my case *all* the time?' she demanded.

It took her five seconds to run up the stairs. Two more to slam her bedroom door.

And that would be the last he saw of her, that evening.

He didn't have a clue what to do now. Stephanie had made it clear that it was his turn to deal with their daughter, and being a full-time dad was as much of a shock to the system for him as it was for Caitlin. Of course he understood that it was hard starting at a new school and being away from the friends you'd known since you were a toddler, but Caitlin had been in London for a month now and things still hadn't got any better.

He'd rather face doing the most complicated and high-risk spinal surgery for twenty-four hours straight than face his teenage daughter. At least in Theatre he had some clue what he was doing, whereas here he was just a big fat failure. He didn't know what to do to make things better. When he'd tried asking her, she'd just rolled her eyes, said he was clueless, stomped upstairs and slammed her bedroom door.

Why was parenting a teenage girl so much harder than the job he'd trained for more than ten years to do?

And how was he ever going to learn to get it right?

He grabbed his mobile phone and headed out to the back garden. Hopefully Caitlin would be less likely to overhear this particular conversation if he was outside; he didn't want her to misunderstand and think he was complaining about her. And then he called his ex-wife.

'What now?' was Stephanie's snapped greeting.

He sighed inwardly. Caitlin had definitely inherited her mother's hostile attitude towards him. 'How are you, Steph?'

'Fine.' She sounded suspicious. 'Why are you calling?'

'Because I need help,' he admitted. 'I'm absolutely rubbish at this parenting business.'

'You can't send her back here,' Stephanie said. 'Not after the way she's been with Craig.'

'I know.' Caitlin had been just as hostile towards Nate's now-ex-girlfriend. Though, if he was honest with himself, the relationship with Georgina had been on its last legs anyway. If the final row hadn't been over Caitlin, it would've been about something else, and he was pretty sure they would've broken up by now. Maybe Stephanie's new marriage had slightly firmer foundations. For her sake, he hoped so. 'I don't know what to say to her. How to get through to her. All she does is roll her eyes at me and slam her bedroom door.'

'She's a teenage girl.'

'I know, but they're not all like that. Not all the time. And she wasn't like that when she visited me or I came down to Devon.'

'So it's my fault?'

'No. I don't want to fight with you, Steph.'

'But you're judging me for putting my relationship before her.'

'No, I'm not,' he said tiredly. 'Who am I to judge, when I put my career before both of you?'

'I'm glad you can see that now,' Stephanie said.

Nate told himself silently not to rise to the bait. It was an old argument and there were no winners.

'Well, you'll just have to keep trying. Because she can't come back here,' Stephanie warned. 'She's your daughter, too, and it's your turn to look after her.'

'Yeah.' Nate knew that asking his ex for help had been a long shot. Given that Stephanie had spent the last ten years hating him for letting her down, of course she wouldn't make this easy for him now. And he knew that most of the fault was his. He hadn't been there enough when Stephanie had been struggling with a demanding toddler, and he hadn't supported her as much as he should have… It wasn't surprising that she'd walked out and taken the baby halfway across the country with her.

Maybe he should've sucked it up and gone after her. Or at least moved closer so that access to their daughter wasn't so difficult. Even though he had a sneaking suspicion that Stephanie would've moved again if he'd done that.

In the end they'd compromised, with Nate doing his best to support his daughter and ex-wife financially by working hard and rising as fast as he could through the ranks. He'd called Caitlin twice a week, trying to speak to her before her bedtime even when he was at work, and then as soon as video calling became available he'd used that—though Steph had made pointed comments about him being the 'fun parent' buying their daughter expensive technology. But without that he would've been limited to the odd weekend and visits in the school holidays. He hadn't bought the tablet to score points or rub in the fact that he was making good money—he'd simply wanted to see his daughter as much as he could, even though they lived so far apart.

'Thanks anyway,' he said, hoping that Stephanie would take it for the anodyne and polite comment it was rather than assume that he was being sarcastic and combative, and ended the call.

Being a new single dad to a teen was the most frustrating, awkward thing he'd ever done in his life.

But he'd have to find a way to make this work. For all their sakes.

CHAPTER TWO

NATE HAD DARK shadows under his eyes, Erin noticed. And, although he was being completely professional with their patients, she could see the suppressed misery in his eyes.

I shouldn't bring my baggage to work.

His words from the previous day echoed in her head. Right at that moment, it looked to her as if he was fighting a losing battle. Clearly whatever was bothering him had stopped him getting a decent night's sleep.

OK, so he'd rebuffed her yesterday when she'd offered to listen. But that didn't mean she should give up on him. Erin knew what it was like to be in a bad place—and she'd been lucky enough to have her best friend's mother to bat her corner when she'd really needed it. Maybe Nate didn't have someone in his life like Rachel. So maybe, just maybe, she could help.

Which would be a kind of payback. Something to help lessen the guilt that would never go away.

At the end of their rounds, she said, 'Can we have a quick word?'

He looked confused, but shrugged. 'Sure. What can I do for you?'

'Shall we talk over lunch?' she suggested. 'My shout.'

He frowned, suspicion creeping in to his expression. 'Is this anything to do with the sensory garden?'

'Absolutely not. No strings,' she promised. 'A sandwich and coffee in the staff canteen. And no haranguing you about my pet project. Just something I wanted to run by you.'

'OK. See you in my office at, what, half-past twelve?' he suggested. 'Though obviously that depends on our patients. One of them might need some extra time.'

She liked the fact that even though he was clearly struggling to deal with his personal life, he was still putting his patients first. 'That'd be great. I'll come and collect you.'

Erin spent the rest of the morning in clinic, and

to her relief everything ran on time. Nate's presurgery consultations had clearly also gone well, because he was sitting at his desk in his office when she turned up at half-past twelve.

'I'll just save my file,' he said, and tapped a few buttons on his computer keyboard while she waited.

In the staff canteen, she bought them both a sandwich and coffee, plus a blueberry muffin, and directed him to find them a quiet table in the corner.

'Cake?' he asked when she turned up at their table.

'Absolutely. Cake makes everything better,' she said.

'So what can I do for you?' he asked, looking slightly wary.

'Yesterday, you said that you didn't know me.'

He winced. 'Sorry. That was rude. I didn't mean it to sound as mean as that.'

'I'm not trying to make you feel bad about what you said,' she said. 'What I mean is that we all go through times when we can't see the wood for the trees, and sometimes it helps to talk to someone who's completely not connected with the situation—someone who might have a completely different viewpoint.'

He didn't look convinced.

'So I guess I'm repeating my offer from yesterday,' she finished.

'That's very kind of you, but—' he began.

'Don't say no,' she broke in. 'Just eat your lunch and think about it.'

'Why are you being so kind?' he asked. 'Because you don't know me, either.'

'I don't have any weird ulterior motive,' she said. 'It's kind of payback. You know—what goes around, comes around. In the past, I was in a tough situation when I really needed to talk to someone. I was lucky, because someone was there for me. So now it's my turn to be that person for someone else.'

'As in me?' He looked thoughtful. 'Got you.'

Though she noticed that he still looked worried. And she could guess why. 'For the record,' she said gently, 'I'm not a gossip. Whatever you say to me will go nowhere else. And right now I think you really do need to talk to someone, because you look like hell.'

He smiled, then. 'And you tell it like it is.'

She shrugged. 'It's the easiest way. So just eat your cake and think about it, yes?'

Nate knew that he really didn't deserve this. But, oh, it was so tempting to take up Erin's offer. If nothing else, she might help him to see things from Caitlin's point of view so he could understand what was going on in his daughter's head. Since Caitlin had come to live with him, he'd never felt more alone.

He believed Erin when she said she wasn't a gossip. He'd never heard her talk about other people in the staff room in their absence. Besides, the kind of people who organised departmental evenings out and collections for gifts for colleagues weren't the kind of people who took pleasure in tearing people down.

Even though he barely knew her, he had the strongest feeling that he could trust her.

And maybe she had a point. Talking to someone who didn't know either of them might help him see his way through this. Then maybe he could be the father Caitlin so clearly needed. 'You're sure about this?' he asked. 'Because it's a long story and it's not pretty. I...' He dragged in a breath. 'Right now, I don't like myself very much.'

'Nothing's beautiful all the time, and if you have regrets about a situation then it's proof that you're willing to consider making changes to improve things,' she said. 'And it might not be as bad as you think. Try me.'

'Thank you.' But where did he start? 'It's my daughter,' he said eventually.

'You're a new dad?' she asked. 'Well, that would explain the shadows under your eyes. Not enough sleep, thanks to your newborn.'

He gave her a wry smile. 'Yes to the sleepless nights bit—but it's complicated.'

She simply spread her hands and smiled back, giving him space to make sense of things in his own head rather than barging in with questions. Funny how that made it so much easier to talk to her.

'I'm sort of a new dad, but Caitlin's not a new-born,' he explained. 'She's thirteen.'

Nate had a thirteen-year-old daughter.

So did that mean he was married? Well, good, Erin thought. That would make him absolutely out of bounds. Any relationship between them would have to be strictly platonic. She was aware that made her a coward, choosing to spend her time with people she knew were unavailable so were therefore safe: but she'd turned her life round now and she wasn't going to risk letting everything go off track again.

But then again, he'd just said he was a new dad. How? Was he fostering the girl?

Giving him a barrage of questions would be the quickest way to make him close up again; but silence would be just as bad. 'Thirteen's a tough age,' she said, hoping that she didn't sound judgemental.

'And she doesn't get on with her mother's new husband.'

New husband? Oh, help. So Nate wasn't married, then—or, at least, he wasn't married to the mother of his daughter.

'She didn't get on with my now ex-girlfriend, either.'

Meaning that Nate was single. Which in turn meant he was no longer safe. Erin masked her burgeoning dismay with a kind smile.

'And I have absolutely no idea how to connect with my daughter.' He sighed. 'Anyone would think I was eighty-five, not thirty-five.'

So if Caitlin was thirteen now, Nate had been quite young when she was born. Not even fully qualified as a doctor, let alone as a surgeon.

Clearly her thoughts showed in her expression, as he sighed again. 'I'm sure you've already done the maths and worked out that we had Caitlin when we were young. Too young, really. Steph was twenty-one and I was twenty-two. We hadn't actually planned to have Caitlin at that point, but we didn't want the alternative, so we got married. We thought at the time it would work out because we loved each other and we'd manage to muddle through it together.'

Yeah. Erin knew that one. Except loving someone wasn't always enough to make things work out. Particularly when the feelings weren't the same on both sides. And particularly when you were too young to realise that it took more strength to let go than to hold on and hope you could change the other person, instead of making the sensible decision to walk away before things got seriously messy. She'd learned that the hard way.

But this wasn't about her baggage. It was about helping Nate.

'It's pretty hard to cope with normal life when you're a junior doctor,' she said, 'let alone a baby.'

'Tell me about it,' he said ruefully. 'I was working—well, you know yourself the hours you work when you're a junior doctor. So I was too tired to take over baby duties from Steph when I got home from work. She'd had to put her plans on hold. Instead of doing a postgraduate course to train as a teacher, she was stuck at home with the baby all day and every day, so I totally understand why she was fed up with me. I should've done a lot more and supported her better.'

'You were working long hours and studying as well. All you can do is your best,' Erin said.

'I tried, but it wasn't enough. Steph left me in the end, when Caitlin was three. They moved away.' He grimaced. 'I should've moved with them instead of staying in London.'

'You're a spinal surgeon,' Erin pointed out. 'There aren't spinal units in every single hospital in the country, and you were, what, twenty-five when she left?' At his nod, she continued, 'Back then you would still have been studying for your surgeon's exams. Even if you'd found another spinal unit close to wherever Steph and Caitlin had moved, there's no guarantee they would've had a training place for you. It's not like working in an emergency department or in maternity, where there's a bit more flexibility and you can move hospitals a little more easily if you have to.'

'It's still my fault. Maybe I specialised too soon, or I should've just stopped being selfish and realised I couldn't follow my dreams. Maybe I should've compromised by moving specialties and working in the emergency department instead,' he said. 'Steph and Caitlin ended up living in Devon, a five-hour drive from me. So I got to see her on the odd weekend, and she used to come and stay with me sometimes in the holidays, but that's nothing like living with someone all the time. I feel as if we're almost strangers. And she hates living with me.'

'So why is she living with you? Is her mum ill?'

'No.' He winced. 'As I said, she didn't get on with her mum's new husband. Steph said Caitlin's a nightmare teenager and it was about time I did my share of parenting—so she sent Caitlin to live with me.'

Erin went cold.

A difficult teenager who didn't get on with her mother's new man, kicked out of home by her mother and sent to live with her father. Erin knew that story well. Had lived through every second of it in misery herself, thirteen years ago. 'When did this happen?'

'Just over a month ago.'

A few days before he'd started his new job. Not great timing for either of them. And now Erin understood exactly why Nate didn't socialise with the team. He needed to spend the time with his daughter and build their relationship properly.

'So she's moved somewhere she doesn't know,

miles away from all her friends and everyone she's grown up with, and she's got to settle in to a new school as well.'

'Which would be a huge change for anyone,' he agreed, 'but it's harder still when you're thirteen years old. And I'm clueless, Erin. I don't know how to deal with this. I'm way out of my depth. I asked Steph what to do, and...' He stopped abruptly.

Clearly his ex hadn't been able to help much. Or maybe she hadn't been willing to offer advice. Erin knew that one first-hand, too. Erin's mother had washed her hands of her, the day she'd kicked Erin out. And even now, all these years later, their relationship was difficult.

But Erin liked the fact that Nate was clearly trying hard to be fair and shoulder his share of the blame for things going wrong, rather than refusing to accept any responsibility and claiming that it was all his ex's fault. 'It sounds to me as if you need a friend—someone's who's been there and understands thirteen-year-old girls,' she said carefully.

He blinked. 'You're telling me you have a thir-teen-year-old? But you don't look old enough.'

'I'm not.' Though she flinched inwardly. If things had been a little different, she might have had a thirteen-year-old daughter herself right now. But things were as they were. And she still felt a mixture of regret and relief and guilt when she thought about the miscarriage. Regret for a little life that hadn't really had a chance to start, for the baby she'd never got to know; relief, be-cause when she looked back she knew she hadn't been mature enough to be a mum at the age of sixteen; and guilt, because she had friends who'd be fantastic parents and were having trouble con-ceiving, whereas she'd fallen pregnant the very first time she'd had sex. The miscarriage had been her wake-up call, and she'd turned her life round. Studied hard. Passed all her exams, the second time round. Become a doctor. Tried to make a difference and to make up for her mis-takes. Not that she would ever be able to make up for the biggest one.

She pushed the thoughts away. *Not now.* 'I was a thirteen-year-old girl once. Although I was a couple of years older than your Caitlin when my parents split up, my mum got involved with someone I loathed and it got a bit messy.' That was the understatement of the year. 'So I ended up living with my dad.' Because her mum hadn't believed her about Creepy Leonard, Erin had gone even further off the rails—and then she'd made the terrible mistake that had ruined her brother's life.

Maybe, just maybe, this could be her chance for payback. To help Nate's daughter and stop Caitlin making the same mistakes that Erin herself had made.

'So you've actually been in Caitlin's shoes?' Nate asked, looking surprised.

'From what you've just told me, pretty much,' Erin said.

He sucked in a breath. 'I know this is a big ask—because you don't know me, either—but, as you clearly have a much better idea than I do about what she's going through, would you be able to help me, so I don't make things even worse than they are for her right now?'

'I'm not perfect,' she warned, 'but yes, I'm happy to try. Maybe we could meet up at the weekend and do something together, so Caitlin can start getting to know me and I can try and get her talking a bit.'

'Thank you.' He looked at her. 'And what can I do for you in return?'

She flapped a dismissive hand. 'You don't need to do anything.'

'If you help me, then I need to help you. It's only fair.'

She couldn't resist teasing him. 'So if I asked you to do a stint in the sensory garden with a bit of weeding or what have you, you'd do it?'

'If that's what you want, sure.' He paused. 'Why is the garden so important to you?'

It sounded as if he actually wanted to know, rather than criticising her. And he'd shared something with her; maybe he'd feel less awkward about that if she shared something in return. Not the whole story, but enough of the bare bones to stop him asking more questions. 'Because I know someone who had a really bad car accident and ended up in a wheelchair. He was helped by a sensory garden,' she said. 'It was the thing that stopped him going off the edge.'

'Fair enough,' he said. 'Don't take this the wrong way but, if you're going to help Caitlin and me, I need to ask you something. Is there a husband or a boyfriend who might have a problem with you doing that?'

'No.'

'OK. I just...' He blew out a breath. 'Well, I've messed up enough of my own relationships. I don't want to mess up anyone else's as well.'

She smiled. 'Not a problem. There's nothing to mess up.'

'Good.' He grimaced. 'And that sounded bad. I didn't mean it like that. I'm not coming on to you, Erin. I split up with my last girlfriend nearly a month ago, a few days after Caitlin arrived, and frankly I don't have room in my life for a relationship. All my time's taken up learning to be a dad, and right now I'm not making a very good job of it.'

'I know you're not coming on to me,' she said. Besides, even if he was, it wouldn't work out. Love didn't last. She'd seen it first-hand—her own parents' marriage and subsequent relationships splintering, her brother's girlfriend dumping him when he needed her most, and then none of her own relationships since her teens had lasted for more than a few months. She'd given up on love. 'I'm focused on my career and I'm not looking for a relationship, either. But I can always use a friend, and it sounds as if you and Caitlin could, too.'

'Yes. We could.' He looked at her. 'I ought to warn you in advance that most of her communications with me right now involve slammed doors or rolled eyes.'

'You need a bit of time to get used to each other and to get to know each other better,' Erin said. 'As you say, seeing someone at weekends and holidays isn't the same as living with them all the time. She needs to find out where her new boundaries are. Her whole life's changed and she probably thinks it's her fault she's been sent to live with you. Especially if she was close to her mum and now they're not getting on so well. What's the problem with her mum's new man?'

'He seems a bit of a jerk,' Nate said. 'Which isn't me saying that I'm jealous and I want Steph back—we stopped loving each other years ago, and the best I can hope for is that we can be civil to each other for Caitlin's sake. But he doesn't seem to be making a lot of effort with Caitlin.'

'If you get involved with someone who has a child, you know they come as a package and you have to try to get on with your new partner's child if you want it to work,' Erin said. 'If Steph's new man doesn't bother doing that, that makes it tricky for you. You can't take sides, because whichever one you pick you'll be in the wrong. If you take Steph's side, Caitlin will resent you for it; and if you take Caitlin's side, Steph will resent you for it. So your best bet would be to tell them both that you're staying neutral, that the bone of contention about Steph's new man is strictly between them, and absolutely refuse to discuss it with either of them.'

He leaned back and gave her a look of pure admiration. 'How come you're so wise? Are you twice as old as you look?'

'And have a portrait of an ageing person in the attic, like Dorian Grey?' she asked with a grin. 'No. I'm twenty-nine.' But if she'd had a portrait in the attic, it would've been very ugly indeed. A portrait of sheer selfishness. She'd spent the last thirteen years trying and failing to make up for it.

'Twenty-nine. So you're just about young enough to remember what it was like, being thirteen years old.'

'And a girl,' she reminded him. 'You're at a disadvantage, you know, having a Y chromosome.'

'Tell me about it.' He rolled his eyes.

She laughed. 'I think you might've learned that particular move from your daughter. I hereby award you a gold star for eye-rolling.'

'Why, thank you,' he teased back.

Nate hadn't felt this light-hearted in what felt like for ever. Not since that first phone call from Steph, informing him that Caitlin was coming to live with him permanently as from that weekend and he had to sort out her new school immediately.

'Thank you,' he said. 'And I'm sorry we got off on the wrong foot.'

'Over the sensory garden?' She shrugged. 'We agreed to disagree. And we're fine as colleagues. I like the way you explain things to patients, and I like the fact you don't look down at Theatre staff.'

'Of course I don't. I couldn't operate without them,' he said. 'Literally.'

'Which isn't how your predecessor saw things, believe me,' she said. 'You'll be fine. It's hard enough to settle in to a new team, but to do it when your home life's going through massive changes as well—that's a lot to ask of anyone.'

'Maybe. I'm sorry if people think I've been snooty.'

'Just a little standoffish. Shy, even.' She smiled. 'They're a nice bunch. And they don't judge. Obviously I'm not going to tell anyone what you've said to me, but if you feel like opening up at any time you'd get a good response. There are enough parents in the department who could give you a few tips on handling teenagers, though I think the big one is to stock up on cake and chocolate. That's what my best friend's mum did, anyway.'

'And do you get on with your parents now?'

Tricky question. Erin knew that her mother still didn't believe her about Creepy Leonard, and blamed Erin for the break-up of that relationship as well as for what had happened to Mikey.

'We get along,' she said carefully. Which was true enough. She and her mother managed to be coolly civil to each other on the rare occasions they accidentally met. But neither of her parents had been there for her when she'd needed them most; her father had been too cocooned in feeling guilty about leaving his family for someone else, and her mother had already thrown her out. And her brother, Mikey, was already paying the price for helping her earlier.

She'd never forgive herself for it. If she hadn't called him in tears, hadn't confided in him about what had happened to her, he would never have come to her rescue—and he would never have had the accident and ended up in a wheelchair.

'You just do your best,' she said with a bright smile. 'So. You said you saw her at weekends and she stayed with you in the holidays. What sort of things did you do together?'

'Things she finds too babyish now—building sandcastles, or going to the park or the zoo.' He spread his hands. 'And how bad is it that I don't have a clue what my own daughter likes doing?'

'The teen years are hard. You're growing up

and you don't want people to treat you as if you're still a kid—but at the same time you feel awkward around adults. It's not all your fault,' Erin said. 'You said your sister was a deputy head. Can she help?'

'Liza's too far away. She lives in York and Caitlin's only seen her half a dozen times in her life. Though obviously Liza deals with teens every day at work, so I asked her advice. She just said to take it slowly and give it time.'

'That's really good advice.' Erin paused. 'What about your mum?'

He sighed. 'She tries. Caitlin goes to her place after school until I've finished at work and can pick her up. But there's quite a generation gap between them and Caitlin doesn't really talk to her, either.'

'It sounds like a vicious circle—the harder you try, the more distance you end up putting between you all.'

'Yeah. You're right. We need help.' He looked bleak. 'Though I feel bad about burdening you.'

'You're not burdening me. I asked you what was wrong, and I offered to help. I wouldn't have done it if I didn't want to,' she pointed out. 'I remember what it was like for me. And I was difficult at fifteen. Rude, surly, wouldn't let anyone close. I was the original nightmare teenager.'

'And it got better?'

With her dad, at least; though they weren't that close. 'Yes.'

'Thank you,' he said. 'It feels as if you've just taken a massive weight off my shoulders.'

And, oh, when he smiled like that… It made Erin's heart do a funny little flip.

Which was completely inappropriate.

If they'd met at a different time in his life, things might've been different. But he didn't need the extra complications of a relationship—especially with someone who had baggage like hers and didn't believe in love any more.

So platonic it would be. It was all she could offer him. 'That's what friends are for,' she said. 'Though, be warned, you might think the weight's back again plus a bit more, when I've had you weeding and carting heavy stones about and then muscles you've forgotten you had suddenly start to ache like mad.'

'As you say—that's what friends are for.' He smiled again. 'Thanks for lunch. My shout, next.'

'OK. But I'm afraid I have to dash, now—I have clinic,' she said, glancing at her watch.

'And I have Theatre.'

'Want to walk back to the unit with me?' she asked.

He gave her another of those heart-stopping smiles. 'Yes. I'd like that.'

She smiled back. 'Right then, Mr Townsend. Let's go see our patients.'

CHAPTER THREE

WEREN'T FAIRY GODMOTHERS meant to be little old ladies with baby-fine white hair pulled back into a bun, a double chin and a kind smile, who walked around singing, 'Bibbidi, bobbidi, boo'? Nate wondered.

But the one Fate seemed to have sent him was nothing like that. Erin was six years younger than he was. Although she wore her hair caught back in a ponytail at work, it was the colour of ripe corn and the curls that escaped from her ponytail made him think more of a pre-Raphaelite angel's hair, luxuriant and bright. She definitely didn't have a double chin; and, although her smile was kind, it also made his heart flip.

Which wasn't good.

If he'd met Erin at a different time in his life—before Caitlin had come to live with him, perhaps, or maybe after he and Caitlin had established a workable relationship—then he would've been interested in dating her. Very interested.

But right now, all he could offer her was friendship. And it was a relationship where Nate was horribly aware that he was doing most of the taking.

That evening, he said casually to Caitlin, 'We're going out on Saturday.'

She looked at him. 'Why?'

'I'd like you to meet a friend of mine.'

She rolled her eyes at him. 'I don't need to meet the women you date.'

'She's not a date,' he corrected. 'She's a friend. And I think you'll like her.'

Caitlin's expression suggested that she didn't think she would. At all.

'Have a think about where you might like to go,' he said.

'I already know that. Home,' she said.

The word cut him to the quick—the more so because he knew she hadn't said it to hurt him. She really did want to go back to the place where she grew up, where she knew everyone around her. 'I'm sorry,' he said softly. 'That's not an option. And I know it's hard for you to settle in to a place you don't know, living with someone you don't really know that well, and to leave all your friends behind and start all over again in a new school—but I'm trying my best to make it as easy as I can for you, Caitlin.'

Tears shimmered in her eyes. 'It isn't fair.'

'I know. Sometimes life's like that. The only thing you can do is try to make the best of it.' Awkwardly, he tried to hug her, but she wriggled free.

'I have to do my homework.'

'OK. But if you want me for anything, I'm here. I'm your dad, Caitlin. I know I haven't been there enough for you in the past, and I regret that more than I can ever explain, but I'm here for you now. And you come first.'

She made a noncommittal noise and fled.

Had he started to make some progress? Or was this how it was going to be for ever? he wondered.

He just hoped that his fairy godmother would be able to work the same magic on his daughter as she'd worked on him, and could persuade Caitlin to open up a little. To let him be there for her.

'Erin, it's the Emergency Department for you,' Ella, the receptionist, told her.

'Thanks, Ella.' Erin took the phone. 'Erin Leyton speaking. How can I help?'

'It's Joe Norton from the Emergency Department. I've got a patient who came in for an X-ray—but the department sent her through to us because when they'd finished she couldn't stand up, and she can't feel anything from the middle of her chest downwards. I think it might be a prolapsed disc or a spinal cord problem, but we really need a specialist opinion. Would you be able to come down and see her?'

'Sure. I'm on my way now,' Erin said. She put the phone down, grabbed the pen to write on the whiteboard and smiled at the receptionist. 'I'm stating the obvious here—I'm going down to the Emergency Department.' She wrote her whereabouts next to her name on the whiteboard, and was just about to leave the unit when Nate came round the corner.

'Just the man I wanted to see. Are you up to your eyes, or can I borrow you?' she asked.

'What's the problem?'

'The Emergency Department needs our specialist opinion. Our patient might have a spinal cord problem, which would be me; or she might have a prolapsed disc in her neck, which would be you.'

'I'll come with you,' he said.

'Thanks.' She smiled at him and scribbled 'ED with Erin' next to his name on the board.

Downstairs in the Emergency Department, she found Joe Norton and introduced Nate to him. 'Depending on the problem, it could be either one of us, so we're saving a bit of time,' she said.

'Thank you both for coming,' Joe said, looking relieved, and took them through to the patient. 'This is Mrs Watson,' he said. 'Mrs Watson, this is Dr Leyton and Mr Townsend from the spinal unit.'

Erin noticed that Mrs Watson's face was ashen and she was trembling slightly. Clearly her sudden inability to walk had terrified her and she was fearing the worst.

'Dr Norton called us down as we're specialists in the area where he thinks the problem lies—so please don't be scared, because we're here to help,' Erin said gently. 'Mrs Watson, we know some of your medical history already from Dr Norton, but would you like to tell us in your own words about how you've been feeling?'

'Call me Judy,' Mrs Watson said in a shaky voice.

'Judy. I'm Erin and this is Nate. He's a surgeon and I'm a neurologist,' Erin explained, 'so hopefully between us we can sort everything out for you.'

'I'm so scared,' Judy burst out. 'It must be really serious for them to have called you. Does this mean I'm never going to walk again?'

'Not necessarily, so try not to worry,' Erin said.

'I know that's easier said than done,' Nate added, 'but tell us what's been happening, and that will help us to work out what the problem might be and how we can help you.'

'It started a few months ago,' Judy said. 'I kept waking up with my right hand all numb and tingling. I thought I was just lying on my arm in my sleep, so I didn't want to bother the doctor with it. But then I woke up last week feeling a bit fluey—and after that I started getting real pain in my neck and shoulders. I took painkillers, but they didn't do a lot.'

The symptoms were starting to add up for Erin; she glanced at Nate, who mouthed, 'TM?'

She gave the tiniest nod—she'd been thinking transverse myelitis, too—but said to Judy, 'That must've been worrying for you. Did you go to see your doctor about it?'

'Yes, and he said he thought it might be carpal tunnel or it might be a problem with my neck, so he was going to refer me for an X-ray.' Judy bit her lip. 'That's why I came to the hospital today. I thought I was just going to have an X-ray and then everything would be sorted out—but then, when it was over, I couldn't stand up, and I can't feel anything from here down.' She pointed to the middle of her chest. 'Dr Norton said it might be inflamed nerves in my neck, or it might be a prolapsed disc.'

'That's very possible,' Nate said, 'but we need to carry out some more tests to help us narrow everything down. I want to do an MRI scan of your spine—that's a special kind of X-ray using magnets and radio waves, and it doesn't hurt but you do have to lie as still as you can in a kind of tunnel for a few minutes, and it can be a bit noisy. Depending on what the scan shows us, I'd like Erin here to do a lumbar puncture.'

'That's a lot less scary than it sounds,' Erin said. 'It means I'll ask you to lie on your side and I'll put a needle into the space between two bones at the bottom of your spine and draw off a little bit of fluid from around your spine so I can run some tests on it.'

'Does it hurt?'

'No. I'll numb the area with a local anaesthetic first,' Erin said. 'It takes about half an hour, and you can have someone with you if you like.'

Judy bit her lip again. 'Dr Norton said he'd call my husband.'

'Good. I'll make sure the department's contacted him,' Erin said, 'and if you'd rather we waited until he's here before we do any of the tests, that's absolutely fine.'

'I'd like James to be with me, please.' She

dragged in a breath. 'I'm so scared I'm not going to walk ever again.'

'I know it's pretty frightening for you right now,' Erin said, squeezing Judy's hand, 'but until we've done some more tests we can't give you any proper answers about why you can't stand up at the moment or what we can do to treat you. What I think we should do now is take you up to our department and settle you in with a cup of tea, and then we'll wait for your husband to arrive before we do the tests. Is that OK with you?'

Judy nodded.

Erin had a quick word with Joe Norton to explain what they were going to do, and the Emergency Department reception confirmed that James Watson would be there in half an hour and they'd direct him up to the spinal unit.

Once James had arrived and Erin had explained the situation to him, they sent Judy for her scan.

Nate looked at the results on his computer. 'I can't see any signs of a prolapsed disc or any compressive lesions,' he said to Erin.

'I'll need to do a lumbar puncture, then,' she said. 'Obviously I'll get the lab to test for signs of lupus, neurosarcoidosis and Sjögren's as well, but it's looking more and more like TM to me.'

Nate was in Theatre when the results of the lumbar puncture came back. Just as Erin had half expected, Judy's white blood cell counts were elevated, and so was her immunoglobulin G index. So she and Nate had been right from the start. She knew that her patient was waiting anxiously for a diagnosis, and anyway this particular condition was her area rather than Nate's, so she decided not to wait for Nate to come out of Theatre to break the news.

Judy and James looked up anxiously when she walked into the room.

'So do you know what's wrong?' Judy asked.

'Yes. It's something called transverse myelitis,' Erin explained. 'Basically it's a problem caused by inflammation of your spinal cord. It's quite rare so your GP probably hasn't even seen a case before, so I quite understand why he thought it might be a problem with your neck or your carpal tunnel. It's called "transverse" because the swelling's across the width of your spinal cord, and "myelitis" because it's to do with the myelin sheath that covers the nerves in your spine.'

Judy looked stunned. 'How did I get it?'

'Sometimes it's caused by a virus,' Erin said, 'and you did say that you'd felt a bit fluey, so it might've been that. But sometimes there's no reason for it—it just happens.'

'Will she get better?' James asked. 'It's not—well…?'

'The good news is that it's not fatal,' Erin reassured him, guessing what he was worrying about. 'And the even better news is that we can treat the condition. I'll give you a five-day course of steroids, Judy, and that will reduce the inflammation and stop the pain.'

'Steroids? Aren't they the things you hear about sportspeople taking when they cheat?' Judy asked.

'No—those are anabolic steroids, which are a totally different type,' Erin explained. 'The steroids I'll prescribe are the sort that occur naturally in the body and help to beat inflammation—actually, they're the same kind that people take for treating asthma. They'll reduce the pain and swelling, and if they don't help enough we can look at a couple of other treatments as well.'

'How long will it take her to get better?' James asked.

'It does take time and you need to be patient,' Erin warned. 'Usually you start recovering in a couple of months.'

'Months?' Judy looked horrified. 'But we were going on a swimming holiday in Greece in four weeks' time.'

'I'm sorry—you're not going to be well enough for that,' Erin said gently. 'It might be a couple of months before you're back on your feet, and then we find that between three and six months after the episode you'll recover more rapidly. And I do need to warn you that it can take up to a couple of years to make a full recovery.'

'A couple of years?' James blew out a breath, looking shocked. 'OK. Could Judy get it again?'

'Usually TM is a one-time thing,' Erin said. 'About a third of patients make a really good recovery, and a third find they have a slight permanent disability.'

'Which means a third don't recover at all?' Judy asked. 'Do you know which one I'll be?'

Erin squeezed her hand. 'I'll be honest with you—right now, it's too early for us to tell how you'll respond to the treatment. But, as I said, we can start with steroids, we have some other treatments that we can try and we'll get you some physiotherapy with a specialist in neurological cases. The exercises will help you get back on your feet and improve your condition, and it's important that you keep doing them—but you will find that you get tired a bit more easily than usual, so you'll need to build up to things.'

'I can't get my head round this,' Judy said. 'So if this thing's caused by a virus, does that mean James could get it as well?'

'No. TM isn't infectious and it's not heredi-tary,' Erin said. 'I can put you in touch with the local support group, so you can talk to other patients who've had the condition. They can help reassure you that this isn't going to be the end of the world.'

'It feels like it,' Judy said. 'Right now, I can't walk. We can't go on holiday next month—and we were going to start trying for a baby after the holiday. We can't do that now, either, can we?'

'It's not ruled out for ever,' Erin said, 'but, yes, you will need to put that on hold for now.'

A tear trickled down Judy's cheek. 'I feel so useless.'

'You're not useless,' James said immediately. 'It's not your fault you're ill.'

'It's nothing that you did wrong,' Erin reassured her. 'But try not to worry. My best friend's mum always used to say, "Never trouble trouble till trouble troubles you." Right now it's very early days and we need to see how you respond to the initial treatment—and, as I said, if the steroids don't help, there are other treatments we can try. Remember, there's more than a sixty per cent chance you'll either make a full or a partial recovery.'

'And what if I don't recover?' Judy asked quietly.

'Then you'll learn to adapt,' Erin said. 'You'd be surprised how quickly people adapt to a new situation.'

'I guess you see a lot of that, here,' James said.

'With people who've broken their back and what have you.'

'We do,' Erin confirmed. 'I'm not saying it's going to be easy, and a lot of people on this unit do suffer from depression as well as from the physical problem that brought them here in the first place, but we're here to help you as much as we can. We can give you lots of support and help.' She smiled at them. 'And you have each other.'

'But this isn't what you signed up for,' Judy said to James.

'Yes, it is. "In sickness and in health",' he corrected. 'You're still the woman I fell in love with and married. And we're going to get through this, Jude. Together.'

'I'll leave you to talk,' Erin said. 'But if you have any questions, please come and find me. That's what I'm here for, OK?'

Judy nodded, clearly too upset to speak, and Erin left the room.

She sat in the office, writing up her notes, but it was so hard to concentrate. Judy was clearly worried that she wouldn't recover and then her husband would leave her. And, although James had reassured her, the whole thing had brought back a lot of painful memories for Erin. The early days after Mikey's accident, when his girlfriend had walked out, leaving him devastated…

At the rap on the door, she looked up. Nate was leaning against the door jamb. 'Are you OK?' he asked.

'Sure,' she fibbed.

He raised his eyebrows. 'I need a word. Can I borrow you for a bit?'

'OK.'

'Let's go to the canteen.'

She frowned, but closed her file and followed him. He bought them both a coffee and cake, and found them a quiet table.

'What's the cake for?' she asked.

'You look as if you need to talk—and someone very wise once told me that cake makes everything better.'

She smiled at him, recognising her own words. 'Thanks. I probably just need cake.'

'So what's sauce for the gander isn't sauce for the goose, then?'

He had a point, she supposed. But the words stuck in her throat.

'For the record, I don't gossip, either,' he said gently.

She gave him a wry smile. 'I'd pretty much worked that one out for myself.'

'So what's upsetting you?'

She took the easy way out. 'Judy Watson.'

'The lumbar puncture showed more than inflammatory markers?' he asked.

She shook her head. 'No, it's definitely TM. I talked her through the prognosis, but she's not adjusting very well to the idea of not being able to walk, even for a few weeks. She thinks her husband's going to leave her.'

'People adjust to their situations—and sometimes they surprise themselves by how well they cope,' he said.

She had a feeling that he was talking about his own situation, too. 'I'm going to put her in touch with a support group. But this is the really hard bit, coming to terms with what's happened and what it might mean for the future—and for her relationship.'

'This sounds personal, not just about a patient,' he said softly. 'Am I right in guessing that you've been here before?'

'Not with TM.' Maybe she could tell Nate some of the truth. 'My older brother, Mikey, has a T5 injury from a car accident.' She knew Nate would know exactly what that meant: that her brother's trunk and legs had been affected by the injury and, although his arm and hand functions were normal, he needed to use a wheelchair and special equipment.

'Is he the one who you said was helped by a sensory garden?'

She nodded. 'And, yes, before you ask, this is exactly why I work in a spinal unit now. I want to make a difference to other people, the way Mikey's team made a difference to him.'

'When did it happen?'

She couldn't quite bring herself to tell him that. Nate was bright enough to work it out for himself. If she told him it had happened nearly fourteen years ago, he'd make the connection. And if he worked out that that accident was all her fault, he wouldn't let her help him with his daughter.

She wouldn't get the chance to make something right.

'Mikey was twenty,' she said instead. 'He was in the second year of his degree in politics. He lost an awful lot of things that mattered to him—being on the university rowing team, his girlfriend, his planned career.' And she knew she'd never stop feeling guilty about how much she'd taken away from her brother.

'Did he finish his degree?'

'Yes, though he changed career—he's a journalist now. Mainly politics. Unsurprisingly, he's usually the one on the magazine who covers the disability stories.' And she'd been the one to nag him into it. If she could turn her life round and ace her exams, then so could he. She'd visited him every single day—when her mother wasn't there, by mutual agreement—and nagged him until he gave in and agreed to go back to finish his degree.

'So where does the garden fit in?'

'I'd been doing research into spinal injuries and treatments, and I came across something about gardens. One of the rehab places had a project involving a garden, and patients were encouraged to help grow things. According to the early research findings, it made a real difference to the patients' mental attitudes. I talked to Mikey's rehab place to see if they could get him involved with the project or maybe become part of it themselves, and they thought it was a good idea. They arranged for him to go and stay at the other rehab place for a few weeks. I didn't get to see him while he was there, because he was too far away to visit, but we talked on the phone every day and we had email. And I could hear the difference in him, every time we talked. Working on the garden gave him hope that he could still do things and his life wasn't over. It made him think about what he *could* do instead of what he couldn't.'

'Now I get why the sensory garden is so important to you,' he said.

'Yes, though you're right, too, about checking costs—because if it's a pet project, you really want it to work and that's more important to you than how much it costs,' she said. 'Which means you're not always getting the best value for money.'

'Well, hey. Get this. We're almost agreeing about something,' he said with a smile.

'It's the sugar talking,' she retorted.

'Cake makes everything better. You're right.' He eyed the crumbs. 'I might try that on Caitlin.'

'Or get her to help make it. She might be into baking.' She paused. 'Did you talk to her about the weekend?'

'Yes.' He winced. 'Let's just say she wasn't very forthcoming.'

'We can play it by ear. I'll have a think about some different places we could go to, and maybe text you a few ideas to run by her?' she suggested.

'That sounds great. Thank you. I'll do the same and run them by you before I try them out on her.'

'OK.' She paused. 'Thanks for making me come here and eat cake, Nate. I try to keep my personal life separate from work, but sometimes a case brings back the early days with Mikey and it gets to me,' she admitted. 'Judy's worried about her husband leaving her if she can't walk—and that's exactly what happened to Mikey. His girlfriend said she couldn't cope with his disability and she left him.'

Nate winced. 'I'm assuming his girlfriend was around the same age that he was when the accident happened—she was in her second year of uni?'

'Yes.'

'Then she still had a lot of growing up to do.' He paused. 'James Watson seemed pretty supportive when I saw them together. I think Judy's worrying over nothing.'

'Me, too, and I've told her that,' she said. 'But thanks. You've made me feel a bit better.'

'Any time. You've made me feel better, too.'

For a moment, their gazes met; again, Erin felt that funny little flip in the region of her heart. But nothing was going to happen. Nate had too much going on in his life to offer her anything more than friendship. Even if his circumstances had been different, she had too much baggage for a relationship to work between them.

If only she'd made some different choices, all those years ago. If only she hadn't gone to that party with Andrew. If only she'd left when he started pushing her. If only she hadn't called Mikey to come and get her and had called her best friend's mum instead...

But you couldn't change the past. You could only learn from it.

'I'd better finish writing up my notes,' she said. She scribbled her mobile phone number down on a scrap of paper and handed it to him. 'Text me later and I'll send you some ideas.' And maybe thinking up things to do to help Nate bond with Caitlin would help her to smother her guilt again.

'We could go on the London Eye on Saturday,' Nate suggested. 'Or the cable car over the Thames.'

Caitlin remained impassive. Obviously neither of those suggestions appealed to her.

'Or shopping. Apparently there are good shops on Oxford Street.' He named the clothing stores Erin had mentioned as being popular with teenage girls.

'I used to go shopping with my friends,' she said.

Meaning that she didn't want to go shopping

with him? OK. He could see that it wouldn't be cool, hanging round clothes shops with your dad. 'How about a speedboat ride on the Thames?'

Her expression clearly said, *Really?*, with only the scorn a teen could muster.

'I'm very happy to hear your ideas,' he said.

She shrugged. 'Whatever.'

He knew she was hurting, so he wasn't going to make it worse for her by yelling at her. He wanted to get closer to her, not push her away. But how?

She hates all the ideas I suggested, he texted to Erin later.

OK. How about this? It's an escape game. You're locked in a room and you have sixty minutes to get free—you have to work as a team to solve the clues and puzzles. There's a countdown clock.

She sent him a link to the company's website. The more Nate read, the more he liked the sound of it.

That looks like fun, he texted back. But you have to book in advance. I just checked and they're not free on Saturday. Can we do that another time?

Or was he presuming too much, hoping that Erin would spend more time with them?

Definitely do it some other time, was her immediate response. Then his phone pinged with another text.

What about food? We could do Camden Lock—the street market there has something for everyone and we could see who can find the most unusual food stall. Or go and spot movie locations, if you find out what her favourite movies are. Or we could go to Abbey Road and do THAT pose on the crossing.

All things he'd love to do. Georgina had only really liked posh restaurants and parties where he'd been just a tiny bit bored. And she definitely hadn't had the patience to deal with a troubled teen.

But Erin was his friend, he reminded himself. Even though he'd like her to be more than that, it wasn't going to happen. He needed to sort his life out, first, and he really didn't have the right to ask her to wait for him.

I'll check with her, he texted back. Maybe we could go and see a movie. Or a show.

Or Madame Tussauds™, she suggested. Depending on what sort of music and movies she likes. She could take great selfies with the waxworks to send to her friends at home.

Clearly she realised her gaffe as soon as she'd sent the text, because a second one swiftly followed.

I didn't mean it like *that*. I meant to her friends. Her home's with you.

I knew what you meant, he texted back.

The problem was, what she'd written was true. Caitlin didn't think of London as her home. And he didn't know if she ever would. Talk to you later. And thanks.

CHAPTER FOUR

AFTER SEVERAL MORE false starts, Nate and Erin decided to take Caitlin trampolining on Saturday morning. 'Even if she's not in a good mood to start with,' Erin said, 'bouncing about will get her endorphins going. And it's not just jumping on a trampoline. There's an obstacle course and an airbag, and you can play dodgeball—so she can enjoy chucking a ball at you. In fact, she can have a competition with me about who can score the most hits on you.'

'You're a big kid at heart, aren't you?' Nate accused with a grin.

'Oh, yeah.' She grinned back at him. 'And if the trampoline place is as good as I think it's going to be, I'm so organising a departmental night out there.'

'Sounds good. We'll meet you at the Tube™

station tomorrow at ten,' he said. 'What do you have to wear?'

'Anything you can bounce in, so jeans would be a good bet,' she said. 'No jewellery, and you have to wear special jumping socks for safety reasons.'

He grimaced. 'That might be a sticking point.'

'Nope. No socks, no chucking a dodgeball at you. That's the rules,' she said with a wink. 'Trust me on this. She'll do it.'

But when Saturday dawned bright and sunny, Erin was filled with doubts.

Was she doing the right thing?

OK, so this wasn't a *date* date. This was helping out a friend.

But would it help Nate to bond with his daughter, or would she be making things worse?

There was only one way to find out. And please, please, let this work out, she begged silently.

She changed into jeans, a neutral T-shirt and flat shoes, tied her hair back in its usual ponytail, and decided not to bother with make-up. By the time they'd bounced round on the trampolines for an hour, she'd be red-faced and glowing; besides, this wasn't the same as if she was dressing to impress a boyfriend. She didn't need to impress Nate. She knew he wasn't interested in a relationship. Even if he was, she was the last person he needed in his life.

Nate and Caitlin were already waiting at the Tube™ station when Erin arrived. It was the first time she'd seen him dressed casually—at the hospital he was always in a suit or scrubs—and her heart skipped a beat. Right now he looked younger. More approachable. *Touchable.*

Oh, for pity's sake. How inappropriate was that? Today was friends only, not a date, she reminded herself sharply.

Like her father, Caitlin was tall and had dark hair, but her eyes were deep brown rather than blue and she had a slightly olive complexion, which Erin guessed she'd inherited from her mother.

'Caitlin, this is my colleague Dr Leyton. Erin, this is my daughter, Caitlin,' Nate introduced them formally.

Erin held out her hand. 'Good to meet you. Call me Erin,' she invited.

Caitlin said nothing and didn't take her hand. But Erin wasn't in the least put out by the teenager's lack of manners; she could remember only too well feeling awkward, out of place and totally miserable, at that age. Right now she thought Caitlin needed someone to cut her some slack.

'Thanks for agreeing to come trampolining with me,' she said with a smile. 'I've wanted to try this new place for the last two months, ever since it opened, but all my friends say I'm insane and refuse to go with me.'

'I didn't agree. He made me come,' Caitlin said, jerking her head to indicate her father.

'And you think it sounds like hell on earth?' Erin spread her hands. 'Well, I can't guarantee that you'll like the music they play, and I might not either, but I can guarantee that you'll feel good after you've been on the trampolines for a few minutes.' She smiled. 'I could give you a really long lecture about why endorphins are the best thing ever when you're having a bad day, but I'll be kind and spare you the science. Let's just say that I'm looking forward to the dodgeball section, and I was going to challenge you to a competition to see who can score the most hits on your dad.'

'Hmm,' Caitlin said. 'So did you ask me along just so you could get close to him?'

Nate looked horrified. Just as he opened his mouth, clearly planning to tell his daughter off, Erin forestalled him. The last thing he and Caitlin needed right now was a fight.

'Are you asking me if I fancy your dad?' she said, looking Caitlin straight in the eye.

The teenager had the grace to blush. 'I suppose so.'

'Nuh-uh,' Erin said, shaking her head. That wasn't strictly true, but Nate wasn't in a position to start any kind of relationship and even if he was then Erin was the last person he should get involved with. Her relationships never lasted, and with his daughter living with him for the first time in years he needed something stable, not something that was bound to go wrong. 'Walk with me, Caitlin, because I need to explain something to you. Nate, you're not allowed to listen, so you have to walk at least ten paces behind,' she said.

'Why?' he asked, still looking horrified.

'Because this is girl stuff. But if you really want to talk about period pains and things like that…' She waited for him to blush. 'Then be our guest,' she finished, waggling her eyebrows at him.

'Got you. I'll walk ten paces behind,' Nate said swiftly.

'Good boy,' Erin said with a grin, and patted his shoulder before shepherding Caitlin through the barriers to the escalator leading to the platform. 'Now, there are some people in the hospital,' she told Caitlin, 'who call your dad Mr McSexypants.'

'They call him *what*?' Caitlin looked horrified; but to Erin's relief she also caught a glimpse of amusement in the younger girl's eyes.

'Mr McSexypants,' Erin repeated. 'And yes, I know he's not Scots. Don't make me explain that bit.'

'All right, but why Mr? I thought he was a doctor?'

'He is. But he's a surgeon—and when you're a surgeon you can go back to being called Mr or

Ms,' Erin explained. 'So. Now you know. A lot of our colleagues fancy your dad and they think he's one of the most gorgeous men in the hospital. But I don't call him Mr McSexypants.'

'What do you call him?' Caitlin asked, looking interested.

Erin laughed. 'I don't think I should tell you. Not yet. But he's not my type.' Again, that wasn't strictly true, but she was working on a need-to-know basis. Neither Caitlin nor Nate needed to know anything about her feelings right now. 'Now, if you made him blond with longer hair, gorgeous biceps and superhero powers, then we'd be talking.'

'Oh, you mean like...' Caitlin named one of the actors in a popular sci-fi movie series. 'He's nice,' she added, almost shyly.

'Isn't he just?' Erin named a couple more from the same movies. 'Actually, any of them would do nicely. I think some of them might have a waxwork in Madame Tussauds™, if you want to go and have a look some time.'

'Maybe.' Caitlin frowned. 'So if you don't fancy him, why do you want to go out with us?'

'Obviously your dad hasn't told you what I told him in confidence,' Erin said gently, hoping that the girl would pick up that it meant she could trust her father, 'so I'll tell you myself. The reason why is because I've been exactly where you are. I was a couple of years older than you when it happened, but my parents split up and then my mum got involved with a real creep. Things got a bit messy, and she sent me to live with my dad—and then I had to start all over at a new school.'

'Just like me.' Caitlin looked at her. 'So you're here because you feel sorry for me, then?'

'No. It's empathy, not pity. I know how it feels to move home and school when you're a teenager. It's hard to fit in and make friends. You feel lonely—like an alien who doesn't belong. And you feel that everyone you left behind is going to forget you so you won't fit in at home any more, either.'

'Yeah,' Caitlin said feelingly.

'They won't forget you,' Erin said. 'It might feel like it right now, but I promise you I've been there and they won't. You just have to learn to juggle a bit. And I was lucky because, although I wasn't getting on very well with either of my parents at the time, I could talk to my best friend's mum, Rachel. I'm guessing that right now that might not be an option for you.'

'It's not,' Caitlin admitted.

'I'm seeing this as my chance to pay forward what Rachel did for me and stop someone else feeling as lonely and miserable as I did when I was fifteen,' Erin said. 'If you want a friend, someone who's going to listen and let you moan to them when things get you down, but who won't let you wallow in misery—then hello, my name's Erin, I work with your dad and I'm very pleased to meet you.'

'And that's it? You're just being kind to me because someone was kind to you?' Caitlin looked as if she was having difficulty getting her head round the concept.

'That's it,' Erin said. 'But if you'd rather do something for me in return so you don't feel that you owe me anything, then you can always nag your dad about what a great idea the sensory garden is.'

'Sensory garden? Like a little garden where

you have plants that rustle and smell and are all different colours?' Caitlin asked, suddenly looking interested.

'And textures and tastes,' Erin added.

'We had one of those at my junior school. We used to have story-time out there in summer and watch all the butterflies. It was brilliant.'

Erin gave the girl a high five. 'Oh, yes. That's *exactly* what I'm talking about.'

'But why do you need a sensory garden?' she asked. 'Aren't you a surgeon?'

'No. I'm a neurologist,' Erin said. 'I work in the spinal unit. Your dad does the surgery side of things and I do the other side, looking at the way our patients' nervous systems work.'

'But don't all your patients come in because they've had an accident and broken their neck or their spine and it needs fixing?'

'Nope. There are lots of other spinal conditions not caused by accidents—some are just caused by people getting older, and some are caused by viruses. Sometimes we can help patients go back to a normal life without any pain. Sometimes we can't get rid of all the pain or they might end up in a wheelchair because the damage is a little bit too much for us to fix, but then we can help them to adjust to a new life.' Erin smiled. 'That's where my sensory garden comes in.'

'So it's your garden?'

'Strictly speaking, it's a community garden that belongs to the hospital, but it's my pet project and that's where a lot of my spare time is going at the moment,' Erin explained. 'I know it makes a real difference to my patients, being able to be out-side in a garden after they've been stuck inside in a bed for months.' She glanced over Caitlin's head at Nate and mouthed, 'Catch us up—you need to hear this.'

'Did you have much to do with your sensory garden at junior school?' she asked Caitlin.

'We had a gardening club and we were allowed to do little bits. We had a tree nursery,' Caitlin said, 'where we planted acorns. When the trees were three years old someone would come and take them to a local woodland to be planted.'

Nate said, 'I didn't know you liked gardens.'

Caitlin rolled her eyes at him. 'You never asked.

Anyway, you're never home and you never talk to me.'

Erin said, 'Hey, truce. When communications break down, there are always faults on both sides. Right now we're agreeing to disagree, OK?'

'OK,' Caitlin muttered.

'OK,' Nate echoed.

'Good. Caitlin, would I be right in thinking you like plant biology?' Erin asked.

The teenager looked at her father and scowled, and then nodded at Erin. 'If my new school actually *lets* me do biology.'

'I'll make sure they do,' Nate said.

Caitlin looked as if she didn't quite believe that he'd fight her corner for her, but to Erin's relief this time she didn't argue.

'You know what—it's really nice and sunny today, and it'd be a shame to spend a morning like this stuck indoors,' Erin said. 'We could give the trampolining a miss and go and look round Kew Gardens instead, if you like.'

'But you said you wanted to go trampolining,' Caitlin said, looking surprised.

Clearly she wasn't used to her views being

taken into account, poor kid. Erin shrugged. 'We can do trampolining another time—maybe when it's raining. I haven't been to Kew for ages. If you haven't been there before, I think you might enjoy the greenhouses. There's one with about ten different climates—it's amazing.'

'I like the biodomes at the Eden Project,' Caitlin said. 'I've been there on a couple of school trips—we live not far away, in Devon. *Lived*,' she corrected herself, looking miserable.

'London's really not so bad, and there are some amazing gardens in the city,' Erin said. 'In fact, there's a garden right next to the Thames where they have banana trees growing in the middle of a bed of sunflowers. We could go and look at them some time, too. And the Sky Garden. I haven't been there, yet, and it'll be nice to have someone to go with.'

'What's the Sky Garden?'

'How good's your phone?' Erin asked.

Caitlin just sighed.

'That bad? OK.' Erin took hers from her pocket and handed it over. 'Look it up on this. Your job today—apart from eating cake with me, talking plants and making your dad see that sensory gardens are totally awesome—is to make a list of gardens in London that you want to go and see. Then we'll work through your list together over the next few weeks.'

Caitlin's eyes grew round as she looked at Erin's phone. 'But this is the latest...'

'I know. I'm a total tech junkie,' Erin admitted with a grin. 'They give me a hard time about it at work because I always get the newest version on the very first day it comes out. I have been known to queue up outside the shop at stupid o'clock to make sure I get one.'

'But if I drop it...' Caitlin looked worried.

'Then, yes, the screen would probably crack and I'd have to get it fixed, which would be a pain. But I'm trusting you not to drop it. You're thirteen, not a baby,' Erin said briskly. 'OK. We're going to Kew instead of trampolining, so we're taking a different route from our original one. You're looking for the District Line, which is the green one. Go and have a look at the map on the wall and tell me which station we need to change at to get there.'

'OK.' Caitlin carefully put Erin's phone in her pocket to keep it safe, and went over to look at the map of the Tube™ lines on the wall.

'Oh, my God. She's talking to you like I've never heard her talk to my mum or to me—even in the days when she was little and seemed to like being with me. How did you *do* that?' Nate asked, looking impressed.

'I was straight with her,' Erin said. 'I told her I'd been in the same place as her, so we've got something in common. And I just hit lucky with the garden thing.' She wrinkled her nose. 'Sorry. That's going to be a bit difficult for you. I promise I didn't do it to score points off you—it was just the first thing that came into my head.'

'I know you're not scoring points, and it's fine. More than fine.' Nate looked relieved. 'You've just given me something I can do for her. She can have her own patch in my back garden—and my mum loves gardening, so it gives her something in common with my mum as well. You're amazing, Erin.'

She lifted both hands in a 'stop' signal. 'I'm not amazing. I'm just me. And it's very early days.

It's not all going to be plain sailing and you're still going to have fights. But this is a good start and you can build on that—because now you both know you're on the same team, right?'

'Yeah.' Nate swallowed. 'You have no idea how good this feels.'

'It's good for me, too, knowing that I can stop someone feeling as bad as I did at that age,' she said. 'So you don't owe me anything, OK? This is a situation where everybody wins.'

Caitlin came back and recited directions about where they had to go and where they had to change lines.

'Great. You're in charge of getting us there,' Erin said.

'But—' Caitlin looked shocked.

'The best way to learn your way about on the Tube™,' Erin said, 'is to just do it. If you miss your stop, don't worry—all you do is get off at the next station, cross to the other platform and go back the other way. There's only one rule.'

'Rule?' Caitlin looked wary.

'I don't have many rules,' Erin said, 'but they're not negotiable and they're not breakable. If you get on the train and you end up separated from me or your dad, then you get off the train at the very next station and you stay right there on the platform where you get off. Then we can find you easily. Same as if I get on first and I'm separated from you, then you stay where you are on the platform and you get on the next train in exactly that place—then when you get off at the next stop you'll see me as soon as you get out of the doors. Got it?'

'Got it,' Caitlin said.

'Good.'

On the Tube™, Caitlin looked up the Sky Garden and started making a list of other gardens. Then she handed Erin's phone back to her. 'Thanks.' She gave Erin a shy smile.

'No worries. I'll text the list to your dad later, and you as well. Put your number in my phone, then I can text you and you'll have my number.' Erin handed the phone back.

'OK.' Caitlin tapped in her number. 'You're not like I thought you'd be.'

'What, a boring old doctor?' Erin teased.

Caitlin shook her head. 'Not that, but...' She spread her hands. 'You're cool.'

Erin laughed and gave her a high five. 'Thank you. So are you.'

Nate paid for their tickets at Kew, refusing to let Erin go halves, and they wandered round until they found the conservatory with the ten different climates.

In the wet tropic zone, Caitlin went all chatty and told them about a school project she'd done in Geography on rainforests and mangrove swamps. And Nate was stunned to realise that his daughter said more to him in the last quarter of an hour than she had in the whole of the previous week.

Finally, Caitlin was connecting with him again. Better still, she shared his love of science—even if her preference was for plant biology rather than human biology. He'd had no idea because he'd never really talked to her about his work, and he knew he had Erin to thank for this. He caught her eye; she smiled at him and gave him a wink, as if to tell him to relax and say that everything was going to be just fine.

It gave him an odd feeling in the pit of his stomach; but he knew she was doing this for his daughter's sake, not for his. He needed to keep that in mind and not let himself get carried away. The attraction he felt towards her was totally inappropriate.

Caitlin was fascinated by the carnivorous plants. 'Are you using anything like that in your sensory garden, Erin?'

'No, because it's all outdoors at the moment and these kinds of plants wouldn't survive the winter outside,' Erin explained.

'They'd be interesting to look at, though, if you did an inside garden.'

'Could Caitlin be involved with the sensory garden?' Nate asked.

'Sure,' Erin said. 'I can take you to meet the garden designer, if you want, Caitlin. His name is Ed, and he's a really nice guy. He's designed a couple of gardens for the Chelsea Flower Show before now.'

'Is that why you chose him to design your garden?' Caitlin asked.

'Not just because he's a good designer. It's a

charity thing so we have to think about costs as well. Ed offered to do the design for nothing, because his brother had a motorcycle accident and broke his back, and he spent a while in our unit before he got a place in rehab,' Erin explained.

Caitlin looked confused. 'Rehab, because he was on drugs?'

'Rehab, as in teaching him how to adjust to life in a wheelchair and helping him with his physiotherapy,' Nate said.

Caitlin looked at him. 'Did you fix his back?'

'That particular accident happened quite a while before I went to work at the London Victoria,' Nate said, 'but if it happened now then, yes, I would probably be the surgeon.'

'So that's what you do all day, fix broken backs?'

'And necks—though not all of them are fractures. Some are where I take off a bit of bone in the spine to take the pressure off the nerves and stop my patients being in pain.' Nate could hardly believe that Caitlin actually seemed interested in his job. If anyone had suggested that to him even a few days ago, he would've scoffed. But now… Now, it felt as if Erin really was a fairy godmother and was fixing his life.

They enjoyed looking round the waterlily garden, and Erin looked something up on her phone. 'Did you know that the leaves of the giant waterlily span two metres across, and they can take the weight of a baby without sinking?'

'They're amazing,' Caitlin said. 'I'd like to sk—' Then she stopped abruptly.

'You'd like to do what?' Erin asked.

Caitlin shook her head. 'It doesn't matter.'

'Were you going to say "sketch"?' Erin asked.

Caitlin shrugged. 'Mum says art's a waste of time.'

'I don't want to fight with your mum,' Nate said, 'but I often have to draw things to explain to my patients what I'm going to do. Without the drawing, it'd take a lot longer to explain and they might still be worried.'

'So you don't think art's a waste of time?'

'No, and if you're thinking about a career in plant biology you'll probably need to be able to draw for your exams,' he pointed out. Why had he never guessed that she liked art?

'So are you good at drawing?' Caitlin asked.

'I can show you some of my student notes later, if you like,' Nate suggested. 'Then you can tell me whether I'm any good. And if you like looking at art, there are loads of good galleries in London. Maybe we could go some time together.'

'All right,' she said, and Nate felt as if the sun had just come out after a long, lonely winter.

They stopped for a toasted cheese sandwich and a milkshake in the café for lunch.

Nate teased Erin. 'I just know you're going to choose cake and claim it's one of your five a day.'

'Of course it is. Blueberry muffins count as fruit,' Erin retorted. 'Right, Caitlin?'

Caitlin looked bemused. 'But you're a doctor. You're supposed to tell people they're not allowed to eat cake and stuff because it'll make them fat and rot their teeth.'

'Cake,' Erin said, 'is absolutely fine in moderation. And in my professional opinion it makes a lot of things better.'

'Trust her. She's a doctor,' Nate said in a conspiratorial stage whisper.

And Caitlin's grin made his heart feel as if it

had just cracked. He thoroughly enjoyed watching his daughter blossom. He knew there was still a long way to go, but for the last month he'd failed badly at being a full-time dad, and now finally she was responding to him; they could build on this. For the first time, he really felt as if there was hope for him as a parent.

After lunch, they wandered round the gardens to find some of the oldest and biggest trees.

By the hawthorn, Nate said, 'Did you know years ago they used to think it was unlucky to take hawthorn indoors because it meant someone in the household would die?'

'But that's not true, is it?' Caitlin asked.

'No—but there is some science behind it. Did you know that the same chemicals in the scent of hawthorn are also present in decaying corpses?'

'Oh, that's so gross!' But she didn't look appalled; she was actually laughing. Laughing *with* him. Just the way she had as a young child when he'd told her terrible jokes and pushed her on the swings.

This was going to be all right, he thought.

He noticed that Erin was really relaxed with

Caitlin, too, in a way that Georgina never had been. And Erin seemed to be blossoming as much as his daughter in the garden environment. Her grey eyes were almost luminous. Beautiful.

He caught his thoughts and gave himself a mental kick. Yes, he was really attracted to her, but he couldn't act on that attraction. If it went wrong between them, he'd be letting his daughter down again and it would make things awkward between him and Erin at work. He'd already discovered that he liked working with her; he liked her kindness with their patients, the way she was always good-humoured and always seemed to bring out the best in people. Just as she was bringing out the best in his daughter right now.

How could he possibly risk losing that?

And even though an insidious little voice in his head suggested that maybe dating Erin would make his life even better, he squashed it ruthlessly. He couldn't take the risk. So he kept things light and chatty, coming up with outrageous facts that made both Erin and his daughter laugh.

At the end of the day, Caitlin actually let Erin hug her goodbye.

'We'll sort out our garden list,' Erin said, 'and maybe we can do some other stuff together as well.'

'The trampoline thing?' Caitlin asked.

Erin nodded. 'And there's a place where they put you in a locked room and you have an hour to escape. You have to work as a team to sort the clues. It's kind of like a console game, but better. I'm dying to try it out. What do you think?'

'That,' Caitlin said, 'sounds like a lot of fun.' She looked at Nate, as if checking that he wasn't going to scoff at the idea.

'I agree,' he said with a smile. 'We'll have to think up a good team name for us.'

'That's settled, then. We'll add it to the list,' Erin said. 'Oh, and we have to go for a proper afternoon tea.'

'Because cake makes everything better,' Caitlin chorused.

Erin laughed. 'Indeed it does. You're a fast learner. See you soon, Caitlin. I'll see you at work, Nate.'

'Yeah, see you—and thanks for today.' So what did he do now? Shaking hands would seem too formal. He wasn't really the kind of person to give her a high five. Should he hug her? Or would that be too forward?

Right at that point, he thought his social skills were quiet a few rungs lower than his teenage daughter's were.

As if Erin guessed at his awkwardness—or, more likely, it stood out like a beacon—she stepped forward and gave him a hug. 'We can't leave you out of the hugs,' she said. 'You can be an honorary girl today. Right, Caitlin?'

The feel of Erin in his arms made him tingle all over. But her teasing comment was just enough to keep him on the right side of self-control.

'Hmm. My dad as a girl. With very short hair,' Caitlin said.

'And guyliner,' Erin suggested.

'Guyliner?' he asked, totally lost.

Caitlin collapsed into giggles.

'Eyeliner. For men,' Erin explained, her eyes full of mischief. 'Blue would look great with your eyes.'

'I am not wearing eyeliner,' Nate said. 'Blue or any other colour.'

And he wasn't sure whether he was more worried or amused by the conspiratorial look they shared. Or distracted by the fact that Caitlin had actually acknowledged him as her dad.

They'd come what felt like a million miles, today. And it made him feel on top of the world.

Hugging Nate goodbye had seemed like the right thing to do at the time, Erin thought on the way home, but it had left her antsy. She'd been so aware of the warmth of his body and his clean masculine scent.

Worse still, she was really attracted to the man Nate was outside work. The one who could admit his vulnerabilities and shortcomings, but who tried so hard to make it right rather than making everyone else fit round him. It was frighteningly easy to imagine herself with him.

But they were doing this for Caitlin's sake. She couldn't afford to start anything with Nate. If it went wrong—*when*, she amended, because she hadn't made a relationship really work since Andrew—there would be way too much collateral damage. She'd simply have to keep reminding herself that they were friends. Just friends. And she couldn't offer him anything more.

CHAPTER FIVE

ON MONDAY, Nate caught Erin in the staff room at lunchtime. 'Do you have time for a quick update?'

'Over a sandwich in the canteen? Sure.' She smiled at him.

'So how's Judy Watson doing?' he asked when they were settled in the canteen.

'She's starting to feel a bit better, though she's not on her feet yet. I've arranged physio, and spoken to some people from the support group—they're coming to see her this week,' Erin said. 'And James is still reassuring her that they won't split up over her illness.'

'That's good to know.'

'So how's Kevin Bishop doing? Did the spinal spacer work in the way you hoped?'

'Yes—he's walking again, out of pain and full of smiles. Though I've warned him that playing football with his kids has to wait until the physio gives him the go-ahead.'

'You can't blame the poor guy for being impatient, though,' Erin said. 'He's been in pain for so long—and now he can actually move again, of course he'll want to run before he can walk. Anyone would.'

'I guess.' He paused. 'Things are quite a bit better with Caitlin, thanks to you. She showed me her sketchpad yesterday. And it turns out that she really likes my mum's cat, Sooty. It never occurred to me she'd like animals—Steph always refused to have a pet because they caused too much mess, and I guess when Caitlin stayed with me in London we tended to stay at my place, so my mum visited us and Cait never saw the cat. She's drawn a few pictures of the cat—and they're good.' He smiled. 'And I had a word with her school, this morning. She won't be choosing her exam courses until next year, but apparently there's a gardening club and the head of the science department is going to have a chat with her today.'

'That's great,' Erin said, meaning it.

'It's still early days,' he said, 'but I actually feel there's a light at the end of the tunnel and we've got a chance of making it work.' He looked her straight in the eye. 'And it's all thanks to you.'

'Hardly. You're the one actually *making* it work. I'm just helping to facilitate things,' Erin protested.

'If you hadn't hit on gardens as her favourite thing, I don't know if she would ever have started to open up to me,' Nate pointed out. 'I was really sinking, Erin.'

'It was a lucky break, and you might've got there on your own.'

'Seriously. You've made a real difference,' he said quietly, 'and I appreciate it.'

'Any time. She's a nice kid.' Much nicer than Erin herself had been. 'I had a word with Ed, the garden designer. He's here on Thursday. If Caitlin wants to drop in after school, he can talk her through what we're doing here.'

'I'll check with her.' He gave her a wry smile. 'Considering that you and I fell out over that same garden, it's pretty ironic that it's made such a big change to my life.'

'Hey. You've come round to my way of thinking because you know now that I'm right,' she teased. 'Actually, Caitlin's texted me a couple of times. Obviously I'm not going to betray any of her confidences and I'm certainly not going to discuss her with you, but she seems to be settling in a bit more.'

'I wish I'd been a better dad to her in the past instead of focusing on my work. If I could do things differently, I would,' he said, his face sombre. 'I wish I could go back and change things.'

So would I, she thought. *So would I.* 'You can't change the past, Nate,' she said instead. 'You can only learn from it. And you did what you thought was best at the time.'

'I guess.' He lifted his mug to her in a toast. 'To you. Because you've made a massive difference, whether you admit it or not.'

'And to you. Because you're the one making the effort.'

Early on Tuesday afternoon, Nate was called down to the Emergency Department to see a patient who'd crashed while driving without wearing a seatbelt, and had been thrown seventy metres from his car.

'I can't believe the guy could even move his arms and legs after a crash like that,' Doug, the lead paramedic, told Nate. 'He didn't show any signs of serious spinal injury, but given what had happened to him we were very careful when we moved him and we put him on a long spinal board.'

'Good call,' Nate said.

'I sent him for an X-ray and it's unbelievable,' Joe Norton said. 'He's got a broken shoulder and ribs, and punctured a lung. But just look at this. I've never seen anything like this before.'

Nate stared at the picture on the computer, stunned. 'I don't think I've ever seen a fracture dislocation as severe as this. Usually a patient who presents like this is paralysed. And you're telling me that this guy can actually move his arms and legs, Doug?'

'Yes. We've assessed him and he can move all his different muscle groups. His sensation is all intact, too. We're all wondering if he's a secret superhero,' Doug said with a grin. 'I've never seen anything like this in twenty years as a paramedic.'

'He'd better hope that I'm in superhero mode in Theatre,' Nate said. 'I can fix the fracture and realign his spine, but the operation's really high risk and there's a chance that it could cause further neurological injury. If any damage occurs to his spinal nerves during the operation, we're looking at paralysis.' And the patient would definitely be a candidate for Erin's garden. 'Is he up to talking?'

'Yes.' Joe took him over to Barney Mason and introduced him swiftly. 'Barney, this is Nate Townsend, our spinal surgeon consultant. He's the guy who's going to fix your back.'

'You can really fix me? So I'm going to be able to walk again?' Barney asked.

'Right now, we're all amazed you've got any movement at all,' Nate said, showing Barney the X-ray. 'You've fractured your spine and it's dislocated as well, so it's a bit on the complicated side.'

'Can you fix it?'

Nate nodded. 'I'm going to send you for some

MRI scans—that just gives me a little bit more detail than the X-rays do—and then we'll take you up to Theatre. But I do need to warn you that your spine is in a serious condition right now, and the operation carries a high risk that you could end up paralysed.'

'But if I move at all while my back's like this, I'll be paralysed anyway,' Barney said. 'Is that right?'

'Yes.'

'As it is, I'm lucky I'm still alive. The way I see it, I have nothing to lose. Go for it,' Barney said. 'Do whatever you have to do.'

'Can we get in touch with anyone for you so they're here when you wake up?' Nate asked.

Barney grimaced. 'Right now, I can't face the idea of all the nagging.'

'Nagging?' Nate asked, not understanding.

'What idiot drives a car without wearing a seat-belt?' Barney asked. 'I'll never hear the end of it.'

'What happened?' Nate asked.

'I was in a rush to get to a meeting. I was having a screaming row with my girlfriend on the phone at the same time because I had to cancel our date for tonight, so I didn't hear the car beep at me to put my seatbelt on. And then...' He blew out a breath. 'I know I'm lucky to be alive,' he said again, 'let alone in almost one piece. I can't believe I'm even here. I thought I was going to die when I went through the windscreen.'

'I could ring your girlfriend or your mum for you,' Nate suggested. 'And I can tell them as your surgeon that you need calm, peace and quiet to help you recuperate.'

'I guess. But no tears. Please. I hate tears.'

Nate was sure that half of this was bravado and Barney Mason was completely terrified at the idea of becoming paralysed, but he squeezed Barney's hand. 'Got it. Now, I'll need you under a general anaesthetic during the op, and the op's going to last for a few hours.'

'Hours?' Barney looked shocked.

'Hours,' Nate repeated, 'because as well as repairing the damage we'll put a special monitoring system in place to make sure we minimise the risk of causing any damage to your spinal cord while we're fixing you. What I'm going to do is put screws above and below the fracture to act as a kind of scaffold, realign your spine, and then insert rods and a titanium cage so you have a strong structure.'

'So I'm going to have a metal spine, then?'

'In part, yes. The cage and rods will be there permanently. I also need to tell you that you're looking at a few weeks to recover from the op, you'll need to wear a supportive brace around your midriff for three months afterwards, and you'll need a lot of physio to help you get back on your feet. Overall I'd say it'll take about six months to get you back to normal.'

'Six months?' Barney blew out a breath. 'I know I should be grateful I'm not dead, but that sounds like weeks of being stuck staring at the same four walls.'

Nate had heard that before. But now, thanks to Erin, he had an answer for it. 'Not necessarily. There are rehab places where you can go out in the garden and even do some work out there. Yes, you'll be in a wheelchair for at least some of the time, and you're going to have to learn to pace yourself. And you need to do whatever the physio team tells you, or you'll set your progress back and it'll take even longer before you're completely back on your feet.'

'I'm not so good with orders,' Barney said.

'It's your call,' Nate said. 'I guess it depends how quickly you want to get mobile again.'

'Yesterday?' Barney asked hopefully.

Nate smiled. 'I'm pretty good at what I do, but I'm afraid that one's beyond even me. It'll take as long as it takes, and I know how frustrating it is for you that I can't give you a definite answer, but no two people heal in quite the same way.'

While Barney was being prepped for Theatre, Nate organised his team of specialists and ran through exactly what he wanted to do, then called Barney's girlfriend and his mother to fill them in on the situation and explain that Barney was going to be tired and groggy after the op and would need quiet support, but Nate himself would be there to answer any questions they might have. He called his own mother to warn her that he was going to be in Theatre for a complicated op so he'd be late picking up Caitlin, but he'd call as soon as he was about to leave the hospital.

Finally he scrubbed up, ready for the operation.

'I know the monitoring system's a bit unusual—it's what we'd usually use for scoliosis cases—but we need to make sure there isn't any damage to the spinal cord during the op,' he told his team. 'So I want monitors on his brain, electrodes on his spinal cord, and we stimulate the muscles of his foot at regular intervals so we can measure his response and see if anything's affecting his spinal cord—if it is, then we stop and think about how to tweak whatever we're doing. Everyone OK with that?'

'Sure,' they chorused. 'You're the boss.'

'I'm just the one with the scalpel. This is a team effort, and everyone plays an important role,' he reminded them.

The monitoring system worked perfectly, to Nate's relief, leaving him to work quietly and methodically to realign Barney's spine and repair the damage. He inserted the screws, rods and titanium cage.

'Thanks, everyone,' he said when he'd finished the last suture to close the incision site. 'You were all great. Between us, we've given this guy a fighting chance to get back on his feet.' They'd made a real difference to Barney's life. Which was exactly what Nate had trained for; but had the price been too high? Or would he get a chance to fix his relationship with his daughter, the way he'd just fixed a complicated dislocated spinal fracture?

The operation had taken time and patience, which was also what Erin had counselled for fixing things with Caitlin. So maybe the situation with his daughter would work out, too.

And he wasn't going to let himself think too closely about his growing feelings for Erin. He couldn't have it all. He needed to be grateful for what he did have instead of wishing for more.

On Thursday morning, just before ward rounds, Nate took Erin to one side. 'Have a look at this.'

She looked at Barney Mason's X-ray and blinked. 'Ouch—that's really nasty. A fracture *and* a dislocation. I don't think I've seen anything as bad as that before.'

'It's probably the worst one I've seen, too,' Nate admitted.

'Is he going to be OK?' Erin asked.

'Come and see him and tell me what you think.'

She blinked. 'You mean you've already fixed that?'

'With screws, rods and a titanium cage,' he said. 'Actually, it's a shame you were off duty on Tuesday afternoon or I would've asked you to be on the neuro-physiological team in Theatre. But actually that's not why I want you to see him. I want you to talk to him about rehab places.'

'Oh.' She grinned as the penny dropped. 'Would that involve sensory gardens, by any chance?'

He rolled his eyes. 'Yes, Dr Leyton. And, yes, I admit that you were right about all the garden stuff. I've been reading up about it, too, and it surprises me how much difference it does make.'

'Excellent.' She punched his arm. 'I'm glad you're finally admitting it. By the way, speaking of gardens, is Caitlin still OK to meet Ed after school in our garden today?'

He nodded. 'Though I'm in Theatre, so if there are any complications when I'm operating I might not be able to make it.'

'That's not a problem. I'll be there to introduce

them to each other anyway, and I can always stay a bit longer if you need me to.'

'Are you sure?'

'Very sure,' she said. 'I don't have anything planned for this evening.'

'Thanks. I owe you one,' he said.

As he'd half feared, there were complications in Theatre, but Nate knew that Caitlin would be safe and happy with Erin. When he finally scrubbed out and had made sure his patient was settled, he called Erin's mobile phone to find out exactly where they were and went down to meet them.

'Good to meet you, Nate,' Ed said, shaking his hand. 'Your daughter here's got a real affinity with plants. She's made some really good suggestions about the design.'

'That's good,' Nate said with a smile. How did he deal with this? Singing Caitlin's praises would probably embarrass her and make her back away; but at the same time he didn't want her to feel that he was just dismissing her.

Erin came to his rescue. 'We were wondering if Caitlin could join the volunteer team, Nate.

Provided it doesn't interfere with her homework or what have you.'

'And it'd look great on her CV if she decides on a career in horticulture,' Ed added. 'Being involved in a hospital sensory garden is a really big thing.'

Caitlin's eyes were wide with longing. 'Can I?' she asked.

Damping down the wish that she'd call him 'Dad', Nate nodded. 'Sure. Provided you stay on top of your homework.'

'I will,' she promised. And then, to his shock, she hugged him. 'Thanks.'

The combination of that hug and the look of pure approval on Erin's face completely floored him. Nate was relieved that Ed picked up the slack by chatting away about what they could do. He didn't pay much attention to what the garden designer was saying, because all his focus was on Caitlin and Erin: his daughter, and a woman who was growing more important to him by the day.

Was he simply being selfish, wanting to have everything? Or was there a possibility that Erin might see him as more than just a colleague whose life needed fixing? Plus he had no idea how she felt. Did she feel the same attraction towards him? Or did she think that the situation was way too complicated for her to want to take their relationship any further than friendship?

At the weekend, it was raining, so Nate, Erin and Caitlin headed out to the trampoline place. As Nate had half suspected they would, Erin and Caitlin ganged up on him in dodgeball and took great delight in throwing the ball at him and bouncing it to each other for another shot at him.

But then Erin tripped and he caught her.

For a moment, he held her close. He could feel the warmth of her body and the softness of her skin, and she smelled of vanilla and chocolate. Edible.

His mouth went dry as he imagined kissing her.

And when she looked up at him, he could see that her pupils were huge.

So did she feel this same pull towards him? Could anything come of this?

He was just about to dip his head and brush his mouth over hers when he remembered where they were—and that his daughter was standing right next to them. Much as he wanted to kiss Erin, he knew it really wasn't a good idea to do it right here and now. So he set her back on her feet with a grin. 'Given how many times you've hit me with that ball in the last ten minutes, you're very lucky I didn't just let you fall flat on your face, Dr Leyton.'

'Yeah, yeah,' she said, and bounced a ball against his chest with a cheeky grin.

'So much for gratitude,' he grumbled.

Erin threw the ball to Caitlin. 'Actually, I think we're about done now,' she said. 'And, as trampolining burns about a thousand calories an hour, I reckon we've burned enough to have afternoon tea.'

'Bring on the cake,' Nate said. 'And scones. I have a ton of calories to replenish.'

She smiled at him, and his heart felt as if it had done a somersault. Ridiculous. He really needed to keep himself under control. But when they were settled in the café with a platter of sandwiches and a tiered stand full of scones and cakes, he found himself staring at her mouth.

Oh, help.

'Dad?'

Then he became aware that Caitlin was talking to him. 'Sorry. Miles away.' But his daughter was bright and he didn't want her to guess why he was wool-gathering. Thinking swiftly on his feet, he said, 'I was wondering how many of these sandwiches I can eat before you notice that I've scoffed your share.'

'I was saying, Erin's tea is actually nice. She just let me try it.'

'It's passion fruit tea,' Erin added. 'My favourite, after pomegranate.'

It was bright orange and it smelled gorgeous.

'Want to try some?' she asked.

'I think I'll stick to my good old-fashioned breakfast tea,' he said. Because the idea of drinking from a cup where her lips had just touched sent a shiver of pure desire running through him, and he needed to stop this right now.

But it got worse when they started some teasing bickering about the proper way to eat scones, and whether the cream or the jam should go on first. Because then Nate and Erin reached for a scone at the same time and their fingers brushed against each other. Nate's skin tingled where they'd touched, and his whole body felt incredibly aware of hers. Maybe he should've sat next to her instead of opposite her—because then he wouldn't have to look at her and wonder what it would be like to touch his mouth to hers. Then again, sitting next to her would've been just as bad, because then his foot might've ended up brushing against hers...

He needed a cold shower.

But for now, concentrating on his cup of tea would have to do.

The following Tuesday morning, Erin let herself into her brother's flat. 'Hey, Mikey.'

He looked up from his computer. 'Hey, it's my favourite sister.'

'Your only sister,' she corrected.

'But you're still my favourite.' He smiled at her. 'Would that be a box of freshly baked cookies I spy in your hand?'

'I made most of them for the bake sale at work later today, but I earmarked these ones for you,' she said. 'Though you have to save at least one for Louisa. And I've already texted her to say I made cookies, so she'll know if you scoff the lot.'

'True. I'll make us some tea to go with them.' He saved his file, wheeled himself into the kitchen and made tea.

Yet again Erin noticed how matter-of-fact Mikey was about his situation. He didn't let his disability get in the way. Then again, she supposed he'd had fourteen years to get used to being in a wheelchair.

'How's the sensory garden doing?' Mikey asked.

'Really well. The structure's almost there, and we're going to start planting things, next week.'

'Has the new guy at work stopped giving you a hard time about it?'

Erin squirmed. Why had she opened her mouth to her brother about that in the first place? 'Uh-huh.'

'Spill,' he said.

She tried for innocence. 'Spill what?'

'I've known you since you were two hours old,'

he reminded her, 'so you can't flannel me. What's the deal with this guy?'

'There's no deal.' That bit was true. 'Nate and I are friends.'

'As in "just good"?' Mikey asked wryly.

Erin nodded. 'We can't be any more than that.'

'Why not?'

'Because his ex-wife has just sent their thirteen-year-old daughter to live with him.'

Mikey winced in sympathy. 'Ah. I take it you're seeing yourself, from the time when Mum kicked you out?'

'Yes and no. Caitlin's a nice kid, actually. Her mum's new husband isn't quite as bad as Creepy Leonard was. It seems that he just doesn't want the bother of having a teenager around or having to share her mother's attention.'

'And she gets on OK with her dad?'

'It's getting better. We found some common ground between them.' Erin laughed. 'Ironically, it was the sensory garden. So I guess that's why he's had to come round to my way of thinking on the subject.'

Mikey wheeled his chair over to her and gave

her a hug. 'Erin, you don't have to rescue everyone, you know.'

'I'm not trying to rescue anyone,' she fibbed.

'You can't change the past,' he said, 'but you've more than learned from it. I know Mum blames you for what happened, but I don't, and as the one who's actually in the wheelchair then I outrank her in the validity of my opinion.'

'And the political journalist goes back into using long words and a fancy sentence structure,' she teased, wanting him to change the subject.

'Erin.' He took her hand. 'When are you going to forgive yourself, sweetheart?'

She couldn't answer that. Mainly because she was pretty sure the answer was 'never'.

'Look at you. Think how many lives you've made a real difference to at work,' Mikey pointed out. 'If I hadn't had the accident, you might not have become a doctor, let alone a neurologist. The way you were going when you were fifteen, you might have ended up drifting from dead-end job to dead-end job, never settling to anything for long.'

She knew he was right, but she still thought

that the price had been too high. And the fact that he'd been the one to pay it was unacceptable.

'And,' he added gently, 'you might have been the mother of a thirteen-year-old yourself right now—which is another reason why I think you're stepping in to help. This girl is the child you could've had.'

'Mikey, I'm not trying to replace the baby. I came to terms with the miscarriage a long time ago. And you and I both know I was too young anyway to be a mum, back then. I wouldn't have given my daughter a good life.'

Her little girl.

Would her daughter have looked like her? Would she have had the same unruly fair hair, the same dusting of freckles across her nose? Would they have clashed as badly as Erin and her own mother did, or would they have been friends as well as mother and daughter?

When she'd first realised she was pregnant, Erin had been horrified, unable to believe it was true. She'd gone into denial about it and pretended it wasn't happening until her best friend had found her crying in the toilets and taken her home to talk to her mother—and Rachel had really helped her come to terms with it and see that the baby was maybe a gift, a chance to have the parent-child relationship she didn't have with her own parents. Losing that had devastated Erin; once she'd accepted the idea of being pregnant, she'd planned to put her child first, to give her child a feeling of importance and security that she'd never had herself.

It had taken a lot of hard work for her to come to terms with the miscarriage and realise that maybe it was her own second chance, and she could turn her life around.

'You don't know for sure that it would've gone wrong,' Mikey said, 'and things are never that clear-cut. Yes, having the miscarriage meant that you could go on to concentrate on your studies instead of having to drop out; but at the same time you missed out on having a child. I think you're still missing out, because you don't let anyone close enough to date you for more than a couple of months, and settling down really doesn't seem on the cards for you.'

She suppressed the ache. 'Maybe. But be honest about it, Mikey. Relationships don't work for me.'

'Because you don't give them a chance.'

She scoffed. 'You and Rachel are the only people who've ever been there for me. And look what I did to you.'

'I was the one driving,' he reminded her, 'and it was an accident. Have you told this Nate guy what happened?'

She shook her head. 'He knows you had an accident, but he doesn't know it was my fault.' She dragged in a breath. 'And he doesn't know about the baby.' She never talked about the baby to anyone nowadays—except when her brother made her talk about it.

'The accident wasn't your fault,' Mikey said again, 'but maybe you should tell him what happened, and he can make you see that.'

'Or he might run a mile in the opposite direction because he'll see me as a bad influence on Caitlin,' she countered.

'Or,' Mikey said, 'more likely he'll see what a brave, strong woman you are, how you've turned your life around and what a great role model you are for his daughter.'

Erin flapped a dismissive hand. 'That stuff is all on a need-to-know basis, and right now Nate doesn't need to know.'

'So you're scared of his reaction?' he asked perceptively.

Petrified. 'No,' she fibbed.

'So he's *that* important. Interesting. And he's the first man you've actually talked to me about in a long time.' Mikey finished making the tea and handed her a mug. 'Open up to him, Erin. If he deserves you, then he'll understand. And if he doesn't understand, then he's not good enough for you anyway.'

She gave him an awkward hug. 'I love you, Mikey.'

'I love you, too, Erin—but you need to start really living your life.'

'I *am* living my life,' she protested.

He scoffed. 'No, you're not, because you won't let anyone close—partly because of what that bastard Andrew did to you.'

'I had counselling,' she reminded him. 'I came

to terms with it. Not all men are rapists. I've dated since then. I've had sex since then.'

But trying to embarrass her brother into shutting up didn't work. 'You still don't let anyone close,' he pointed out.

She sighed. 'Mikey, love doesn't last. So what's the point in looking for it?'

'Love *does* last,' he said. 'And I can prove it.'

'How?

'Grab your diary, because Louisa and I are taking you out to dinner.'

'Dinner? That sounds good. What's the occasion?'

'Double celebration. I got promoted to editor at the magazine,' he said.

'That's fabulous news! Then I'm buying the champagne at dinner—no arguments,' she said.

'Accepted,' he said with a smile.

'You said double. What's the other bit?' she asked.

'That's the proof I was telling you about. We're looking for a chief bridesmaid,' he said. 'Know anyone who might be interested?'

It took a second for the penny to drop. 'You're getting married?'

He grinned. 'I asked Louisa at the weekend and she said yes. And you're our first choice as chief bridesmaid. Actually,' he confided, 'we're hoping to make it a triple celebration, because we've been accepted for the IVF programme.'

'Mikey, that's wonderful news.' Tears welled in her eyes as she realised that she hadn't quite taken everything away from her brother. He was going to get married to the woman he loved and who loved him in return, and with luck they were going to have a child together.

'So,' he said softly, 'I understand about turning your life round, being brave enough to risk loving someone and letting them love you. And if I don't let being unable to walk get in my way and stop me doing things, then you shouldn't let anything get in your way and stop you doing things, either.'

'I'm not. I'm too busy at work to date.'

'Busy? Sweetheart, what that means is you don't have to take any risks. Working hard and helping others means you're able to hide how vulnerable you are and bury your fears.'

Mikey was too perceptive for her comfort. Which went with the territory of being a political journalist, she supposed—he wasn't afraid to tackle difficult subjects and he didn't let people back away from the truth.

'I'm not one of your interviewees, Mikey. You don't have to give me a hard time. Anyway, I brought you cookies. And they're still warm. Don't let them get cold while you keep yakking on.'

'Hmm. But just think about this, Erin: if you carry on keeping people at a distance, Andrew keeps winning. Is that what you want?' he asked.

'No, but we're not talking about me. We're talking about your wedding.' She lifted her mug of tea. 'Congratulations, Mikey. I'm so pleased for you and Louisa. And if you need any help organising anything at all…'

'You're my wing woman,' he said. 'You always have been. If it wasn't for you, I wouldn't have gone back to finish my degree or had the confidence to apply for my job—or to start dating Louisa.'

'I guess.' But if it hadn't been for her, he would've finished his degree two years earlier and had a completely different life. Why didn't he hate her for taking so much away from him?

'Think about it. Talk to Nate. If he's worthy of you, he'll understand.'

'Yeah.' She finished her tea and kissed him. 'I have to go. The bake sale starts in an hour and a half and I need to set up the stall.' And she knew she was being a coward. Mikey had a point. Taking the risk of a relationship with someone wasn't something she wanted to do. Taking the risk that it would break down, that happiness would be snatched away and yet again she'd lose someone she loved. She couldn't face it. Better not to risk her heart. Better to keep herself busy at work and helping other people, so she didn't have time to think about what she might be missing.

'Go get 'em, kiddo.' He punched her lightly on the shoulder. 'Talk to the guy, and let me know how it goes.'

'I will,' she said, having no intention of doing

either. Nate was her friend. And she didn't want to risk losing that—or the chance to help Caitlin and make sure she didn't repeat Erin's mistakes.

CHAPTER SIX

AT THE HOSPITAL, Erin set up her bake stall in the atrium, where everyone visiting the hospital would be able to see it. Her colleagues on the spinal unit had contributed cakes or cookies, whether home-made or a glitzy one bought from a bakery, as had staff from other departments who knew her well. Volunteers from the Friends of the London Victoria had also brought in cakes and were helping her to man the stall.

'Caitlin sent these. She made them last night,' Nate said, coming along to the stall with a plastic box filled with home-made brownies.

'Awesome. I'm definitely buying one of these,' Erin said with a smile.

'And my mother says to thank you.'

'What for?'

'Because Caitlin asked her if she could bake something, and she wanted to use one of Mum's recipes. Thanks to you, Caitlin's starting to open up to her as well.' He swallowed hard. 'She actually called Mum "Gran" last night, for the first time in months. And she's started calling me "Dad" instead of avoiding the word.'

Erin felt a lump in her throat. 'That's so good to hear.'

'Yeah.' He rested a hand on her arm. 'We owe you.'

Her skin tingled where he touched her, and she had to remind herself that it was inappropriate.

She was busy with the bake stall all afternoon and didn't really have the time to think about Nate, but the question went round and round in the back of her mind: was Mikey right, or would Nate run a mile if she told him the truth about her past? Telling him risked losing his friendship—and she'd lost enough in her life. But at the same time she knew she'd held so much back that their friendship was based on a lie—on who he thought she was, rather than who she really was. That wasn't healthy, either.

She was just packing up when he came over.

'I've finished in Theatre and written up my

notes, so I wondered if you need a hand with anything?' he asked.

'I'm just returning the tables I borrowed from one of the meeting rooms. Don't you need to go and pick up Caitlin?'

'She'll be fine with Mum for a while.'

'Then if you've really got time, sure, you can give me a hand.'

It was fine until they both reached for the same table at the same time and their fingers touched. Erin felt that same prickle of awareness as when their hands had touched over the scones; but this time, instead of avoiding eye contact, she looked him straight in the eye. Nate's pupils were dilated to the point where his eyes looked almost black.

Oh, help. It looked as if this attraction she felt towards him was mutual, then. What were they going to do about it? Because this situation was impossible.

His face was serious. 'Erin.' He reached out and cupped her cheek in his palm, then brushed his thumb over her lower lip.

She felt hot all over and her skin tingled where he touched her.

'Nate. We're right in the middle of the hospital,' she whispered.

'And anyone could see us. I know.' He moved his hand away. 'Erin, I think we need to talk.'

She knew he was right. 'But not here.' It was too public.

'Where? When?' His voice was urgent.

'You said Caitlin would be all right with your mum for a while.' She took a deep breath. Maybe she needed to be brave about this, as Mikey had suggested. Do it now. Tell him the truth. And if he walked away—well, it just proved that she'd been stupid to let him matter to her. 'My place, right now?'

He nodded. 'I'll drive you.'

'No, we need to go separately. We don't want people to start gossiping about us,' she said quickly.

'I guess you're right,' he said.

'I'll text you the address on my way to the Tube™,' she said.

'OK. I'll, um, see you soon, then.'

His eyes were full of longing—the same longing that she felt. But, once he knew the truth about her, would he look at her in a different way?

There was only one way to find out. And it scared the hell out of her. But he'd find out in the end, so she knew it would be better to tell him now. Before either of them got hurt.

Though she had a nasty feeling it was already too late for that.

Nate walked back to his car to wait for Erin to text him her address so he could put the postcode into his satnav, feeling as nervous and excited as a teenager on his first date—which he knew was crazy. They weren't actually dating. They might not ever date. After all, what did he have to offer her apart from a very complicated life?

But the kind of pull he felt towards her was rare, and the way she'd just reacted to him made him think that it might be the same for her. Between them, could they find some kind of compromise?

He really hoped so. Because, the more he got to know Erin, the more he liked her. She was serious when she needed to be, and yet she had a sense of fun and an infectious smile. She was sweet and kind and funny. She was straight-talking and not afraid to face things head-on. And physically he was more aware of her than he had been of anyone since he'd split up from Stephanie ten years before. He wanted her more than he could ever remember wanting anyone.

Erin realised that she was actually shaking with a mixture of nerves and excitement as she got on the Tube™. She wanted this so much—and yet if she thought about it she knew it made no sense at all. Where could their relationship possibly go from here? Nate came as a package, and his relationship with his daughter was still so new and so fragile that he couldn't afford to take his focus away from it. Plus they worked together at the hospital, so if things went wrong between them—given her track record, she amended, that was more likely to be 'when' than 'if'—it could be awkward between them in the department.

So, even if he felt that same pull of attraction, they were just going to have to pretend that it didn't exist. Because this couldn't happen. Once she'd told him the truth about her past, he would realise for himself that she wasn't a good bet and he'd back away. Though, at the same time, part of her didn't want to tell him the truth because she didn't want to risk losing his friendship.

Yet she knew that the longer she left it to tell him, the closer she got to him, the harder it would be to find the words. So she needed to be brave. Tell him. *Now.*

Her flat was reasonably tidy, but she whizzed the Hoover round while the kettle boiled—more to stop herself from thinking than because her flat needed cleaning.

And then the doorbell rang.

Nate.

Erin felt almost sick with nerves, and her heart was beating so hard as she walked to the front door that she was sure people in the street outside could hear it. She took a deep breath, and gave Nate her best and brightest smile. 'Perfect timing. The kettle's just boiled—tea or coffee?'

'Whatever you're having.'

'Coffee,' she said. It would take longer to make and it might buy her enough time to slow her pulse rate and get her common sense back. 'Come and sit down. I won't be long.' She ushered him in to the living room, intending to be all bright and breezy and chirpy—but then he stopped in the doorway and dipped his head to kiss her.

When he lifted his head again, she was shaking.

'Nate, I…' She didn't have a clue what to say. That kiss had just blown her mind.

'Me, too,' he whispered. 'I wasn't expecting this and I know it's unfair of me to do this because I come with complications.'

So did she. And, if this thing between them was to stand even the slightest chance of growing into something good, she needed to be honest with him right from the start. 'Coffee,' she said, and fled to the kitchen.

When she returned with two mugs, he was browsing the photographs on her mantelpiece.

'I take it this is your brother?' he asked, gesturing to the picture of her with Mikey. They were sitting in her father's garden, laughing together, and Mikey's wheelchair was very obvious.

'Yes,' she said quietly. She handed him one of

the mugs and took a deep breath. 'I told you that Mikey's in a wheelchair. What I didn't tell you was that it's my fault he's in a wheelchair. So I guess I owe you an explanation.'

He frowned. 'You don't owe me anything.'

'I think I do—before things between us…' She swallowed hard. 'Well.' Too late to go back, now. She just had to hope that he wouldn't hate her the way her mother did or think that she'd be a bad influence on Caitlin. 'I should probably have told you this before. And, once I've told you the truth about me, I'll understand if you want me to stay out of your life.'

His frown deepened. 'But I do want you in my life, Erin. That's the whole point of us talking now.'

'You need to know the truth about me, first. You know I said my parents split up when I was a couple of years older than Caitlin?' At his nod, she continued, 'When Dad left us, I went off the rails pretty badly and I got in with a rough crowd. I might have found my own way back out of it again—but then my mum started seeing this guy.

Mikey and I called him "Creepy Leonard."' Even thinking about the man made her feel sick.

'Why was he creepy?' Nate asked.

'I always felt that he was watching me. And it wasn't just teenage awkwardness or paranoia. The way he looked at me...' She shivered. 'Let's just say I discovered that he thought that dating the mother meant that he had the same rights over the daughter.'

Nate looked truly shocked, his eyes widening in horror. 'You mean he...?'

'He *tried*,' she said grimly. 'When he touched me inappropriately, I told him to take his disgusting hands off me or I'd scream the place down. Then I kicked him hard enough in the shins to make him let me go.' For a second, she gritted her teeth. Remembering the older man's lecherous behaviour still made her angry. 'He called me a tease, and I told him I was nothing of the kind. I also told him that my boyfriend would beat him up if he ever laid another hand on me.' Considering what had actually happened with Andrew, that was so ironic. But at the time she'd thought that her boyfriend would protect her from all harm. It hadn't occurred to her that Andrew was where the real danger lay.

'Did you tell your mum what he did?'

She nodded. 'But Leonard had got there before me. He'd convinced her that I was trying to stir up trouble so they would split up—and she didn't believe me when I told her what really happened.'

Nate looked as if he couldn't take it in. 'That—that's *appalling*, Erin. Why would she believe the word of a guy she obviously didn't know very well rather than her own daughter?'

'Remember, her life had just fallen apart,' Erin said. On her counsellor's advice she'd tried so, so hard to see it from her mother's point of view; she'd gone over it again and again, trying to work out what her mother had been thinking. 'Her husband of twenty years had just left her for someone else. She felt ugly and useless and old and betrayed, and then this guy flattered her and made her feel good about herself again. Of course she was going to listen to him.'

'Even though he'd just tried to touch her fifteen-year-old daughter very inappropriately?'

'I blamed Mum for Dad leaving us,' Erin said,

'so we weren't getting on very well. She thought I was trying to spoil things for her—that I was trying to get my revenge on her for Dad leaving, by breaking up her relationship with her new man. From a distance of fourteen years, I can understand why she thought that.'

'It's still appalling. You were a child. Why on earth didn't she listen to you and put you first?' Then he looked at her in horror. 'Oh, my God. Erin. You don't think Steph's new husband…?'

'Tried to touch Caitlin inappropriately?' she asked, guessing what was worrying him. 'No. I think he just wants Steph to himself and doesn't want to share her attention with her daughter. Caitlin's opened up to me about some things, and I think she would've told me if there was any more to it than that—which isn't saying you're a bad father,' she added swiftly, 'just that it's a lot easier to tell something difficult like that to someone who isn't your parent.'

'That sounds like personal experience talking.'

'It is.' She blew out a breath. 'My best friend Gill's mum, Rachel—I told her what Creepy Leonard had done, and she said I needed a lock on my bedroom door to keep me safe. She got her husband to fit it for me that same evening. Mum was really angry when she found out. She said I was attention-seeking and trying to cause trouble for Leonard because I was jealous.'

'You were pretty much understating it when you said your relationship with your mother was tricky,' Nate said, still looking shocked.

'Just a bit,' she admitted. 'Anyway, the lock worked, because it kept Creepy Leonard out. But things got even worse between me and Mum after that, and I started spending more and more time with the crowd who accepted me for who I was—even though they weren't good for me and deep down I think I knew that.' She closed her eyes for a moment. 'Nate, I mean it when I said I went off the rails. It was really bad. I started skipping school and hanging out with them instead, and going to parties that were way too old for me. Let me spell it out for you—I was running around with a crowd who drank and smoked and did soft drugs.'

'Did you do what they did?' he asked.

'Not the smoking or the drugs. But I did start

drinking vodka when I wasn't old enough, just so I fitted in with them,' she admitted. 'I was fifteen, but I looked old enough to be eighteen, so I got away with it. And one of my new friends got me some fake ID for when we went clubbing. Let's just say we went to the kind of places where they didn't check the ID that closely.'

'I take it your mum was too caught up in Creepy Leonard to notice what was going on?'

'To be fair,' Erin said, 'even if she had been looking out for me, she wouldn't really have known what was going on because I covered my tracks pretty well and we were barely speaking to each other.' She bit her lip. 'And then one night I went to this party. I wish now I'd never gone in the first place, but I guess it's easy to see things in hindsight.'

'And you were still very young,' he said gently.

'I made some really bad decisions, Nate, and my brother was the one who paid the price for it. I don't think I can ever forgive myself for what I did.' She swallowed hard. This was something she almost never spoke about. 'Nobody at work knows about this.'

'They're not going to hear anything from me,' Nate promised.

'Thank you.' Though that didn't make it any easier to tell him. Every word felt as if it ripped another layer off the top of her scars. But if they were to have any chance of a real relationship, he needed to know who she really was. What she'd done. 'Andrew, my boyfriend, had decided that night was the night we were going all the way.' She closed her eyes for a moment. 'I wasn't ready. I didn't want to do what he wanted, because I wasn't even going to be sixteen for another couple of months, but he was nineteen and he expected me to behave like the rest of the girls in his crowd. He didn't want to wait any longer.'

And she'd been so, so shocked by his reaction at her refusal. By the way he'd pushed her into one of the bedrooms, locked the door behind them and thrown all the coats off the bed. Shoved her onto the mattress. She could still feel the weight of his body on hers, his hands gripping her wrists and holding them above her head. The panic when she'd realised that nobody would be able to hear her scream—and, even worse, that nobody was going to come to her rescue even if they did hear her.

'He said age was just a number and it didn't matter. I said I didn't want to do it, but he wasn't listening. He wanted to have sex with me.' She swallowed hard. 'So he pushed me into one of the bedrooms, locked the door and took what he wanted.'

Nate took the mug from her hand and placed it on the low coffee table next to his own, then drew her over towards the sofa and scooped her onto his lap, holding her close.

'Oh, honey,' he said, his voice gentle. 'What a horrible, horrible thing to happen to you.'

'I guess it was my own fault. I knew what that crowd was like. And we'd—well—I'd let him touch me more intimately than I should've done at that age, and I'd touched him. Even though I knew I wasn't ready... It was good to be accepted by someone. To feel loved again—because I didn't think either of my parents cared about me any more. I really thought Andrew loved me, Nate. He'd been pushing me to go the whole way with him for a while, but I'd held off, and...' Bile rose in her throat, and she grimaced. 'Maybe Creepy Leonard was right and I was a tease who deserved what I got.'

'Absolutely not,' Nate said, and kept his arms wrapped round her. 'No means no, and Andrew should've accepted that and waited until you were ready.' He stroked her cheek. 'Violence doesn't solve anything, but I'd quite like to flatten the guy, right now.'

'Violence *really* doesn't solve anything,' she emphasised. 'That's why Mikey ended up in a wheelchair. After Andrew finally unlocked the door and let me out of that room, I called my brother and asked him to come and get me. I didn't say what Andrew had done, but when Mikey took me home I realised Mum and Creepy Leonard were out, and I just broke down and told him. He said I had to call the police, but first he was going to make absolutely sure Andrew never did that to another girl—and he drove off before I could stop him.' She dragged in a breath. 'On the way back to confront Andrew, Mikey had the accident.'

Nate stroked her hair. 'Erin, it was an *accident*. It wasn't your fault.'

'No? According to my mother, if I hadn't been an attention-seeking whore, Mikey wouldn't have been driving, let alone anywhere near the crash site.' Erin swallowed miserably. 'And she was right.'

'No, she wasn't,' Nate said. 'Erin, we deal all the time with patients who've been paralysed in accidents, and we talk to their relatives. You know how many of the relatives find it hard to accept what's happened and the consequences. Blaming someone for the accident is the only way they can start to come to terms with it. It sounds to me as if that's what your mother was doing, and because you were the closest person to her you were the one who copped the flak.'

Why wouldn't he understand? 'But it's *true*,' Erin said again. 'If I hadn't gone to that party, Andrew wouldn't have forced me to have sex with him, I wouldn't have called Mikey afterwards to rescue me and Mikey wouldn't have ended up in the crash.'

'It's a chain of circumstance, and you can't

know that the crash wouldn't have happened anyway. Mikey could've been driving anywhere, at any time, and still had that crash.' He stroked her face. 'Did you tell your mother about what Andrew did?'

It was another memory that made her flinch. 'I tried.' Erin closed her eyes. 'She said I was making it up, trying to get attention away from Mikey in his hospital bed.'

Nate couldn't suppress a curse. 'What about your dad?'

'Mum sent me to live with him because she couldn't bear the sight of me—because it was my fault Mikey was never going to walk again, and every time she saw me it reminded her of what I'd done.'

'Did you tell your dad about Andrew?'

Erin shook her head. 'I didn't think he'd listen, either. Not that Dad had fights with me, the way Mum did, but he felt guilty about having the affair and leaving us, and he avoided talking about anything emotional. Dad's one of those men who just can't deal with emotional stuff. He simply looks away, mumbles, "All right," and changes the subject.'

'So you were all on your own? What about your friend's mum? Did you tell her?'

'No.' At least, not then. She'd talked to Rachel later, when it was way, way too late. But she couldn't bring herself to tell Nate about that. Telling him this much had drained her emotionally. She didn't have the strength to tell him the bit that had finally broken her.

'So Andrew got away with it?'

'I guess.' She bit her lip. 'I feel bad about that, too, because I hate to think he might have gone on to do the same thing to someone else.'

'Erin, it really wasn't your fault. You were still a child yourself and you needed someone looking out for you, not blaming you.'

She could guess from his expression what he meant. 'Don't judge my mother too harshly,' she said softly. 'She was really upset about what happened to Mikey. And I can see where she was coming from.'

'Has your mother ever seen the situation from your point of view?' Nate asked.

The crunch question. 'No,' Erin admitted. 'But that doesn't matter because I can see hers. And I can't forgive myself for what happened to Mikey, because he wouldn't have been in his car that night if I hadn't asked him to rescue me.'

'What does Mikey say about it?'

'Pretty much what you do,' she said. 'Actually, he's the one who told me I ought to tell you about this.'

'He was right. I'm glad you did.'

'Even though you know now how—' she caught her breath '—how *bad* I am, deep down? You don't think I'm going to be a bad influence on Caitlin?'

'You were young and you made some mistakes,' he said. 'Just because you've made some bad choices, it doesn't mean that you're a bad person.'

Was that true? For the first time ever, Erin thought that maybe there was a chance. Maybe the way she'd lived her life ever since had started to make up for her actions as a teen.

'If you were talking to someone who'd been in

your situation, would you judge them as harshly as you judge yourself?' he asked.

She thought about it. 'Maybe not.'

'Definitely not,' he said, 'because you'd see that circumstances played a big part in what happened. It's very clear to me that you can see similarities with Caitlin's situation and your own,' Nate continued. 'You've persuaded Caitlin to talk to you and trust you, so you can guide her into not making the same kind of mistakes that you did.'

She looked away. 'So you think I'm using your daughter to try and stop myself feeling guilty?' Which she was, in a way. Which made her hate herself even more.

'No. I think you're being a strong, kind woman who's using her experience to stop someone else going off the rails in a similar situation. Isn't it time you stopped beating yourself up about the past?' he asked. 'What you went through was terrible. Erin, your parents both abandoned you at a time when you needed a bit of support, you had to deal with your mum's new man behaving inappropriately towards you and then you were raped by the boyfriend you believed loved you. The fact you've managed to get through all that and you've become a doctor who makes a real difference to people's lives—you're amazing, Erin.'

'I don't feel amazing,' she said. 'And don't try to sugar-coat it. I didn't behave well when I was fifteen. I was rude, surly and uncooperative. I drank alcohol when I was under age, and I went to clubs with a fake ID. I skipped school and I failed every single one of my exams.' Between the shock of Mikey's accident and finding out that she was pregnant, and then losing the baby, she'd given up. She hadn't even seen any point in turning up to write her name on the exam paper. So she'd stayed at home, curled in a ball underneath her duvet and crying about the wreckage of her life.

'That was then. Half a lifetime ago,' he said. 'You're a different person now, and it's the you of today I want to get to know better.'

Nate really still wanted to know her? Even after what she'd done?

Hope bloomed in her heart.

She knew she ought to tell him the rest of it—about the baby and the miscarriage—but right now she was too raw.

'But.'

Ah. She'd known it was too good to be true. This was where he'd do the 'it's not you, it's me' speech. He'd take the blame, to make her feel better—but he'd still leave her. Just as she'd always thought: relationships didn't work for her.

'The thing is,' he said, 'Caitlin needs all my attention right now. I want to get to know you better, Erin, and to date you properly, but I don't see how that can happen for a while. Not until Caitlin's really settled. It's not fair of me to ask you to wait for me for an unspecified amount of time.'

He was right. She couldn't complain. Especially as she agreed with him. Completely. 'You're right about Caitlin. She needs you,' Erin said. 'And I—well, everything that happened means I don't tend to get too deeply involved with anyone.'

'Because you blame yourself and you don't think you're worth loving?'

She flinched. 'You don't pull your punches, Nate.'

'Neither do you. But you *are* worth loving, Erin. If things were different...'

'Yeah.' She knew that one well. It was a line she'd used herself, often enough, to get out of emotional involvement. To back away rather than being the one who was rejected.

'Or,' he said, 'we can try something.'

'Such as?' She couldn't quite let herself hope.

'Let's look at it logically. You don't want to date anyone, because you can't forgive yourself for a mistake you made when you were fifteen—half a lifetime ago. When you were still a *child*, Erin. I don't want to date anyone, because I've already made enough mistakes where my daughter's concerned and I need to put her first.'

'Uh-huh.' He'd summed it up pretty fairly.

'So maybe,' he said, 'we can date in secret.'

'Date in secret?' she asked. How on earth could he think that was a logical solution?

'Nobody else needs to know about this,' he explained. 'Just you and me. No pressure. We take it at our own pace and see where things go between us.'

'You really want to date me?'

'I really want to date you,' he confirmed, his blue eyes full of sincerity.

She blew out a breath. 'Even though you know the truth about me now?'

'Even more so,' he said. 'So, you and me. How about it?'

'I...' She stared at him. 'I don't know what to say.'

He pressed a kiss into her palm and folded her fingers over it. 'No strings attached, Erin. We simply go on dates and get to know each other better.'

'How are we going to find time to date, between work and Caitlin?'

'Maybe we can snatch a little time between work and home,' he said. 'I didn't say it was going to be conventional dating. It'll probably be breakfast out rather than dinner, or a snatched coffee here and there, or a walk in the park. But we can still make time for each other and get to know each other properly.' He paused. 'If you want to.'

Oh, she wanted to. So much. He was the first man in years to make her want to take a risk.

And if he was prepared to take the risk, too… She smiled, then. 'OK. Let's give it a go.'

'Good.' He stroked her face. 'We'll take the pace at one you're comfortable with. And I hope you realise that I'll listen to you—if you say no, then as far as I'm concerned you mean it and I'm not going to push you.'

She knew he meant it, and tears pricked at the back of her eyes. 'Thank you.'

'Have you ever dated anyone since Andrew?' he asked.

She'd already told him that. And that she'd kept her relationships very short. But she also knew that wasn't quite what he meant. 'You mean, have I had sex with anyone since I was raped?'

He raised an eyebrow. 'What was that you were saying about not pulling punches?'

'I guess,' she said wryly. 'To answer your question, yes, I have. I had counselling, thanks to my best friend's mum. I told Rachel in the end, but there was no point in going to the police because it was too late to have any evidence. But she got me to go to counselling to help me come to terms with it all. She even went with me to the first appointment. And I've had full relationships since. I just haven't wanted to get too deeply involved, that's all.'

'I'm sorry that you had to go through such a rough time,' he said gently.

She shrugged. 'Don't they say that whatever doesn't kill you makes you stronger?'

'You,' he said, 'are an incredibly strong woman, and I really admire your courage. And I'm glad you trusted me enough to tell me about your past.'

'I'm glad, too.' It felt as if the weight of the world had been lifted from her shoulders. And it was the first time in years that she'd actually felt hope about any kind of relationship.

He kissed her cheek, and her skin tingled at the touch of his lips. 'Given that you've just told me something so painful, I really don't want to leave you. I don't want you to think I'm just abandoning you. But—'

'—you need to collect Caitlin,' she finished. 'It's OK. I understand, Nate. You come as a package.'

'I don't want you thinking that I'm just grabbing the first excuse to scarper and then you won't see me for dust. Because I *do* want to date you, Erin. I want to get to know you better. And I want you to get to know me. Not just as a surgeon or as Caitlin's clueless dad who really needs help to connect with his daughter, but the real me.'

'Yeah.' She kissed the corner of his mouth, then slid off his lap. 'Go and collect Caitlin. I'll see you at work tomorrow.'

He stood up. 'I'll wash up my mug before—'

'No, it's fine,' she cut in with a smile. 'I know you're house-trained. You don't have to prove anything to me.'

'I guess.' He tucked a strand of hair behind her ear. 'I was going to say, seeing you makes me feel like a teenager again. But I guess your memories of being a teen are pretty unhappy, so that isn't tactful.'

'Other people had nicer teenage years than I did,' she said. 'But I'm not angry about it. Envious sometimes, I admit. But life is what it is, and you just learn to make the best of it.'

'Maybe,' he said, 'I can make you feel like the way you make me feel. Like a teenager, but in a good way.'

'Start a brand new slate.' And oh, how she wished that could be possible.

'Something like that.' He kissed the tip of her nose. 'If anything I do makes you uncomfortable, tell me, because I'm not a mind-reader.'

'You're doing pretty well so far,' she said.

'Good. I'll see you tomorrow. Though I reserve the right to send you soppy texts in the meantime.'

She laughed, then. 'I can't imagine the formal, slightly snooty surgeon I first met sending soppy texts to anyone. Or even Caitlin's clueless dad, because he wouldn't even know where to start with textspeak and the kind of acronyms teenagers use.'

'That,' he said, 'was a definite gauntlet you've just thrown down. Keep your phone on. I'll respond to that challenge later tonight.'

And his smile made her feel warm all the way through.

He stole one last kiss. 'Later.'

It was a promise. And one she knew he'd keep.

CHAPTER SEVEN

Roses are red, violets are blue, I can't write rhymes but I really like you :)

IF ANYONE HAD told Erin that Nate could write the kind of verses beloved of teenage boys—and would send them to her in a text, complete with a smiley face—she would never have believed them.

But his text made her smile for the rest of the evening.

You, too, she texted back.

Am in late on Friday, he added. Can you make breakfast?

Well, that was direct.

Sure. Let me know what you want me to cook.

He called her immediately. 'Sorry, I didn't mean I was expecting you to cook breakfast for me. I meant, if you could make it, I'd like to take you out to breakfast. You know, dating stuff?'

'Out for breakfast? How very decadent of you, Mr Townsend,' she teased. 'Thank you. That would be lovely.'

'Do you know anywhere nice that's not too far from the hospital?'

'But far enough away to keep us safe from the hospital grapevine?' she suggested.

'Got it in one.'

She could practically hear the smile in his voice. 'Yes. I'll text you the address and I'll meet you there. What time?'

'I'll drop Caitlin to school first. Give me time for traffic. Say, nine?' he suggested.

'Nine's perfect.'

'Good. See you tomorrow. Sweet dreams.'

'You, too.'

At work the next morning, they kept things completely normal between them. They did ward rounds together, then discussed a case where one of her patients needed to talk through the possible surgical options. As far as everyone else on the ward was concerned, Nate and Erin were simply colleagues. But she could see from the expression in his eyes that he didn't think of her as just a colleague any more. She didn't think of him that way, either.

And she couldn't wait for their breakfast date.

On Thursday afternoon, after her shift, Erin met Caitlin at the sensory garden as they'd arranged to do on alternate Thursdays; they worked together, then had a hot chocolate in the hospital canteen while they waited for Nate to finish his shift.

'School's asked me to do a photo diary for their website,' Caitlin told her proudly.

'Good idea. Maybe you could do an article for the hospital website, too,' Erin suggested. 'I could ask the PR team for you, if you like.'

'I know you're too young to be thinking about that sort of thing now, but it'll look great on your CV. Go for it,' Ed added with a smile. 'Right. Come and see these plants with me, and you can ask me whatever you like about why I've chosen those particular plants for those particular locations.'

Caitlin beamed at him and grabbed her notebook.

Nate sent Erin another text that evening.

Roses are red, violets are blue, my daughter's smiling, it's all down to you.

Not just me, she texted back. You have a lot to do with it. And Caitlin herself.

We'll agree to disagree, Nate said, though you'll admit I'm right eventually.

Yeah, yeah. See you for breakfast tomorrow.

He'd said that she made him feel like a teenager again—and she understood what he meant. That breathless excitement, that sense of wonder and expectation and hope. Her own teenage years had been much darker, but maybe he could bring that lightness back to her life.

Though doubts stomped through her all the way to the café, the following morning. What if he'd changed his mind and didn't turn up? Or, worse still, if he did turn up and then told her he didn't want to see her as more than a colleague in future? Or what if she really messed this up, the way she'd messed up all her past relationships?

But when Erin walked into the café Nate was already there, waiting for her in one of the booths and skimming through the menu. He looked up and smiled at her and her heart skipped a beat. If he could be brave enough to turn up simply because he wanted to date her, then she could be brave, too. So she walked up to him, kissed him lightly on the mouth and slid into the booth opposite him. 'Good morning, Mr Townsend.'

'Roses are red, violets are blue, you look beautiful…and you just kissed me, so I can't think of a rhyme,' he finished.

'That's incredibly feeble, Nate,' she said, laughing. 'I know you can do better than that.'

'All the words fell out of my head, the moment you walked into the room,' he said. 'I told you that you make me feel like a teenager.'

'Hmm.' She smiled, and he handed the menu to her.

'My treat. Whatever you want.'

'Thank you.' When the waitress came over, she ordered eggs Florentine, a skinny cappuccino and a glass of water.

'The hollandaise sauce cancels out the healthiness of the spinach, you know,' he teased.

She laughed. 'I don't care. It's my favourite breakfast ever.'

'Bacon sandwich with tomato ketchup all the way for me,' he said with a smile.

'Me, hunter,' she teased back.

And then, once their breakfast arrived, the conversation stalled.

'This is ridiculous,' Nate said. 'We've worked together for a couple of months. We've been out together with Caitlin a couple of times. We know we can talk for hours because we've already done that. So why do I not have a clue what to say to you right now? Why do I feel as if a toddler has better social skills than I do?'

'Because this is different,' she said. 'It's a proper date. We know the rules at work, and when we've gone out with Caitlin. Whereas dating...'

'It's all new stuff we have to negotiate,' he agreed. 'Risky.'

'Yeah. I haven't dated in a while. I can't quite remember how to behave,' she admitted.

'I made a real mess of my last relationship,' he said. 'So that makes two of us.' He reached across the table and squeezed her hand. 'Didn't we agree earlier that there weren't any rules? That we were just going to take it as it comes?'

'We're just not very good at actually doing that,' she said.

He laughed. 'I guess. Maybe we ought to pretend we're at work.'

'Just not discussing our patients,' she agreed.

Weirdly, admitting their doubts was the thing that made the atmosphere between them easy again, and she found herself relaxing with him until it was time for them to leave for the hospital.

He paid the bill, then walked outside the café hand in hand with her. 'I take it we're going to the ward separately?'

'Indeed we are.'

He kissed her lightly. 'I wish we weren't at

work so we could spend the day together and do something. I want to date you properly, Erin.'

'We agreed it'd be an unconventional court-ship,' she reminded him, 'and that's fine. We'll cope.' She kissed him briefly. 'I'll see you at work.'

Again they managed to behave as if they were colleagues only, when they were at the hospital; though when they were in a meeting together Nate pressed his foot lightly against Erin's under the table. She glanced at him and the sheer desire in his eyes made her catch her breath.

Could this work out?

Could they really have it all?

Or was she setting herself up for the biggest fall ever?

'Oh, you are joking.' Nate groaned when he walked onto the ward on Monday morning and saw the newspaper article pinned up on the notice board. *'Local hero builds Barney's new back'*, said the headline. And there was a photograph of Nate, in a suit, looking serious. 'Where did this come from?' he asked.

'Local paper,' Ella, the receptionist, told him with a smile. 'You're famous.'

'But I didn't talk to anyone—or give anyone a photo.'

'Must've been the hospital PR team who gave everything to them,' she said. 'But it's a good photo. Of course, this means that you're now our official departmental pin-up.'

Nate groaned again. 'I am so not a pin-up. Or a hero. I'm just a surgeon—part of the team, like everybody else.'

He just about managed to live down all the ribbing at work; but when he went to pick up Caitlin from his mother's house, she waved the article at him. 'Gran found this today,' she said. 'You're in the paper, Dad!'

He sighed. 'Just ignore the headlines, Cait. I'm not a hero. I'm simply one part of a big team who fixed Barney's back. I just did my job. It's what I trained to do.'

'It's still impressive,' his mother said. 'That photograph of that poor man's X-ray—it looked more like a jigsaw puzzle than a spine. There aren't many people who can do what you do, Nathaniel.'

'Hmm,' he said, rolling his eyes. 'It's my job, that's all.'

He thought that was the end of it until Ella from their reception desk patched a phone call through to his office on Thursday afternoon.

'Dr Townsend? I'm sorry to bother you at work. It's Jenny Olland, Caitlin's form tutor.'

Nate went cold. 'Is she all right?'

'She's absolutely fine,' Jenny reassured him. 'She's settled in a lot better now. No, I'm calling you because I'm also her Personal Development teacher. I gave my students an essay to write, this week, on the subject of "my hero", and Caitlin wrote hers on you.'

'On me?' Nate was so shocked that if he hadn't already been sitting down he would've fallen over.

'Yes. She included the article about you from the local paper. And I was thinking—we like to have a range of people coming in to school to talk to our students. I think they'd find you inspiring. Would you be able to come in and give our students a talk about your job at one of the assemblies?'

Nate was still trying to get his head round the fact that Caitlin had written an essay about her hero—and it was about *him*. 'I, um—do you mind if I talk it over with Caitlin first?' He needed to be sure that she was comfortable with the idea before he agreed. The last thing he wanted to do was to ruin all the progress they'd made by embarrassing her and making her feel awkward in front of her new friends.

'Of course, Dr Townsend.'

'I'll call you tomorrow,' he promised.

When he replaced the receiver, he stared at his computer screen, not seeing the X-rays or his patient's notes. He couldn't quite believe that phone call had just happened.

Then he was aware that someone was knocking on his open door. He looked up to see Erin standing there.

'Are you OK, Nate?' she asked.

'I… No, not really,' he admitted. 'That was Caitlin's form tutor.'

Erin frowned and came over to his desk. 'Oh,

dear. Is there a problem at school? Anything I can do to help?'

He explained what had just happened, and she reached over to squeeze his hand. 'That's *brilliant*. I'm so pleased.'

'I can't quite get my head round it,' he said.

'Be proud,' she advised.

'I am. And thrilled. And shocked. And I never thought...' His voice tailed off and he shook his head, all out of words to describe how he felt right then.

'I know,' she said softly. 'But you deserve it. You've put the effort in with her. What are you going to do?'

'Talk to her about it,' he said. 'If she wants me to do it, I will—if she doesn't, I'll make up an excuse.'

'Good plan,' she said.

'Sorry, did you want me for something?' he asked.

'No. I was just passing and saw that you looked a bit shocked,' she said. 'But, now you come to mention it...' She lowered her voice. 'How about breakfast, tomorrow? My treat?'

Odd how planning a secret date with her made his heart beat faster. And Nate was pretty sure it was the same for her, given that her eyes were almost black instead of grey right now. 'Same time, same place?' he suggested, keeping his voice equally low.

'Perfect,' she said. 'Catch you later. Let me know how it goes with Caitlin.'

He caught up with his daughter later that afternoon in the sensory garden, during her weekly roster session.

'You planted that whole section?' he asked.

She nodded. 'I think I did it right. Nola—she's the one in charge today—is going to come and have a look at it in a minute and let me know if it's OK.'

'It looks good to me,' he said. 'By the way, Miss Olland rang me today. She told me about your essay.'

Caitlin went pink and stared at the ground. 'Oh.'

'I can't believe you wrote that essay about me.'

She bit her lip, looking anxious. 'Did I do wrong?'

'No.' The lump in his throat was so big that it almost blocked his words. 'I'm thrilled that you did that—though I did tell you I'm not a hero, Caitlin. I'm just doing my job here and I'm trying to be the best dad to you I can be, and we both know I'm still not very good at it.'

She shuffled her feet and looked awkward.

'Miss Olland asked me to come in and talk to the school about my job.'

Her eyes widened. 'What did you say?'

'That I'd check with you first,' he said. 'If you want me to come in and do the talk, I'll do it. But if it'll be embarrassing to have me at school, then I'll tell them I'm sorry, I can't make it due to pressure of work. I said I'd give her an answer tomorrow, so think about what you'd rather I do.'

'OK.'

'Would you, um, like to come in and see where I work?' he asked.

Her smile almost broke his heart. 'Yes—what, now?'

'When you've finished here.'

'I'm finished, if Nola says it's OK. I just need to check with her and wash my hands.'

They went in search of Nola, who inspected Caitlin's work and pronounced it first class. Nate showed his daughter to the nearest washroom and waited outside until she was ready. Then he took her up to see the theatre where he operated, and finally the ward, introducing her to his colleagues who were on duty.

'You've got a photo of me on your desk,' she said when he showed her his office.

'Well—yes. Do you mind?' he asked.

'No. I…' She swallowed and shook her head. 'It's nothing.'

'Tell me.'

She looked away. 'Mum said you never really wanted me,' she said. 'That's why I didn't want to come and live with you.'

He could've shaken Steph for that until her teeth rattled. How mean was it to use their child to score points off him? But Steph wasn't the important one here; Caitlin was. He wrapped his arms round her and hugged her fiercely. 'Of course I wanted you, Cait! I admit, we didn't plan to have you, but I was so thrilled when I found out I was going to be a dad. I went to every single scan and every single antenatal class with your mother—I changed my shifts at work to make sure I was there. I know your mum and I didn't manage to make it work, and I probably should have moved to Devon and changed my specialty so I could see more of you.'

'But then you wouldn't have been able to fix people like you do now.'

'True, but you're the one who paid the price of me putting my job first, and I regret that so much. I wanted to have a good job so I could support you and your mum—but really you needed me to be around more, not just a voice on the phone or a face on a video call, or someone you saw for just a couple of days at a time. I thought I was doing the right thing, though now I know I wasn't and I'm so sorry that I got it wrong. I've still got a lot to learn about being a dad but, Cait, I'm really glad you're living with me now and I'm so proud of you.'

She hugged him back. 'I'm glad I'm living with you, too.'

Nate felt as if his whole world had just turned full Technicolor™. And he knew it was all thanks to Erin that Caitlin finally seemed to have accepted him.

Erin.

His secret date.

Would Caitlin accept her as more than just a friend?

But it was way too soon to ask that kind of question. He'd promised that he wouldn't rush Erin and the same was true of his daughter, too. So he'd just have to take things slowly. Even though he was pretty sure where his feelings were going.

Erin was waiting for him in the café, the next morning.

'I think we should adopt this one as "our" booth,' he said, sliding in opposite her.

'Sounds good to me.' She smiled at him, and his heart felt as if it had just done a triple somersault.

'Hey. Good morning.' He leaned over the table to kiss her; and he kept his hand entwined with hers as they looked through the menu and argued over the merit of pancakes versus croissants.

'So what did Caitlin think about you doing a talk at school?' Erin asked when their breakfast arrived.

'She's thinking about it,' he said. 'I have a feeling she's probably going to talk to her friends about it today.'

'Good idea,' Erin said. 'And it's great that she's settling in better.'

'I know she really enjoys her alternate Thursdays when she works with you on the sensory garden,' he said.

'Me, too. She's a nice kid. And I'm not just saying it because she's yours.'

'She likes you,' Nate said.

Erin smiled. 'It's mutual. And it's important to have an adult friend who can listen to you.' She wrinkled her nose. 'Sorry. I'm overcompensating. I guess it comes of growing up with parents who didn't connect with me,' she said.

He shook his head. 'Don't ever change, Erin. I like you exactly as you are.'

'Same goes for you,' she said. 'Now you've got over being a grumpy old man about the garden.'

'Yeah, yeah.' He liked the way she teased him, too, and stopped him being over-serious.

And all too soon it was time for them to leave for work. He'd definitely have to figure out a way to snatch more time with her, he thought. He'd just need to be a little more creative.

Nate did the talk at Caitlin's school assembly the following Wednesday, having asked permission of some of his patients to use their X-rays as examples and taking along a model of a spine.

He was surprised by how much he enjoyed talking to Caitlin's year group—especially when he'd finished the talk and threw the floor open to questions.

'So people who've been paralysed—can you do all that robotic stuff to make them walk again?' one of the children asked.

Nate knew exactly what the boy was talking about; the case had hit the headlines in some of the national papers recently. 'We don't do that in our hospital at the moment, and I'm a spinal surgeon rather than a neurosurgeon,' he explained. 'But there's some research in America where they've been working on a kind of neural bypass, so the neurosurgeons can transmit signals from someone's brain to electrodes in their knees.'

'Making them into a human robot?' the boy asked. 'A cyborg?'

'Sort of,' Nate said with a smile. 'It's especially amazing because the nerves of the spinal cord can't regenerate. In the research report I read, the patient needed support from a harness and a walking frame to stop him falling, but he did actually manage to walk on his own—after years of being paralysed. It gives a lot of hope for people in the future.'

'The paper said you're a hero and you built that man a metal spine,' one of the girls said.

'I built him a kind of metal scaffold around his spine so it can heal without any pressure on it and so he doesn't have to stay lying down until the fractures heal,' Nate explained. 'And what the paper forgot to say was that I'm only one part of the team. Everyone's important in Theatre, from the anaesthetist to the nurses, and without them I couldn't do any operations. As far as I'm concerned, I'm not a hero. I'm part of a team.'

'So being a surgeon—does that take longer than being a normal doctor?' another asked.

Nate nodded. 'Once you've done your degree and your two foundation years, you need to keep studying for another set of exams. It takes a lot of dedication and sometimes you have to make sacrifices—and so does your family. But it means you can make a real difference to people's lives and I can't think of any other job I'd rather do.'

'Even though there's a lot of blood?' one of the children asked.

Nate grinned. 'Yeah. You get used to that bit fairly early on.'

At the end of the assembly, he said goodbye to the children and the teachers and headed back to the hospital. Erin was in clinic all morning so he didn't get to see her until lunchtime, when they grabbed some sandwiches from the kiosk outside the canteen and headed to the park.

'So how did your talk go?' she asked.

'It was good,' he said. 'Some of the boys were really interested in the robotics stuff.'

'The neural bypass and electrodes in the knees?' she asked, looking wistful. 'Yeah. If we ever get a chance to do a research project like that…'

'Mikey?' he asked softly.

'If I could help my brother walk again, and give him back everything I took away…' She swallowed. 'Yeah.'

'Everything the accident took away,' he corrected, and twined his fingers through hers. 'And, from what you told me, he already lives his life to the full. He just got that promotion, he's getting married and he and his fiancée have been accepted onto the IVF programme.'

'Which is all good stuff, I know.'

'He's forgiven you. Why can't you forgive yourself?' Nate asked.

'Habit, maybe. I'll try harder,' she said lightly. She looked at him. 'I hate to remind you, but we're in the park opposite the hospital. We could see someone we know, any second now.'

Regretfully, he disentangled his hand from hers. 'Yeah. Sorry. Right now I really, really want to kiss you. But you're right. This is too public.'

'Later,' she promised.

'I'll hold you to that, Dr Leyton,' he said.

And funny how even the idea of kissing her made the day feel that much brighter.

He's forgiven you. Why can't you forgive yourself?

Erin had brushed it aside when Nate had said it, but she thought about it all evening. Was she using her guilt as an excuse, so she didn't have to risk trusting someone—or letting someone trust her?

Yet she was letting Caitlin trust her.

And Nate trusted her with his daughter.

If they could trust her, then surely she could trust herself not to mess this up and let them both down?

But she wasn't the only one to think about in this relationship. There was Nate. And Caitlin. Both of them were vulnerable, in different ways. Caitlin saw her as a friend—but would she be able to accept Erin as Nate's girlfriend? Especially since her mother's new husband had rejected her; and Caitlin had told Erin privately that her dad's ex-girlfriend had made her feel as if she was a nuisance and in the way.

Then again, Caitlin knew that Erin had been in her shoes as a teen, and would never put anyone else in that position. And after those first couple of outings, Erin had encouraged Nate to take Caitlin out on his own, using work as an excuse not to join them—it was important that the father-daughter bond didn't rely on someone else being the glue.

Erin blew out a breath. There were no easy answers. For now, she'd take each day as it came and just enjoy her stolen moments with Nate.

CHAPTER EIGHT

ON WEDNESDAY, Joe Norton called up to Erin. 'We've got a patient coming in with a spinal cord injury, in about ten minutes. The paramedics say that she's bradycardic, but her blood pressure's through the roof. We could really do with an expert opinion.'

'Sure—I'll come down. Would the spinal injury be T6 or above?' Erin asked. 'And the injury was less than a year ago?'

'I'll check the file. Yes, T5 and six months ago,' Joe confirmed. 'How did you know?'

'Because it sounds to me like autonomic dysreflexia,' she explained. 'I'll come down.'

'Everything OK?' Nate asked as she put the phone down.

'Emergency department—sounds like a patient with AD,' she said.

He smiled at her. 'Your side of things, then, not mine—so you don't need me to join you.'

'Not this time,' she said with a smile. 'See you later.'

By the time she'd gone down to the emergency department and explained about the condition to Joe Norton, the patient had been brought in.

'Kiki Lomax, aged thirty-five,' Doug, the paramedic, explained. 'Her blood pressure's high, she's got a pounding headache on both sides, her chest feels tight and her heart rate's on the low side. I've given her medication for her blood pressure, loosened her clothing and kept her sitting up.'

'Exactly the right stuff,' Erin said with a smile. 'Thanks, Doug. Kiki, hello—I remember when you first came in to the spinal unit,' Erin added. 'I don't know if you remember me, but I'm Erin Leyton.'

'Yes, I remember you,' Kiki said.

'How are you feeling, apart from the headache and the tightness in your chest?' Erin asked.

'Sweaty and hot on my top half, but cold on my lower half,' Kiki said.

'I had a feeling you were going to say that. You have something called autonomic dysreflexia. It happens quite often to someone with your kind of injury, and we can fix it,' Erin reassured her.

'Autonomic dys...?' Kiki frowned.

'Dysreflexia,' Erin repeated. 'Or AD for short. Your autonomic system is part of your nervous system. It's the bit that regulates your blood pressure, breathing and digestion. What happens is that something below the level of your injury is irritating your system and sending messages through your nerves up to your spinal cord. The messages travel upwards until they reach the site of your injury, and that's where they get blocked. That starts off a reflex from your nervous system that narrows your blood vessels and makes your blood pressure rise. The receptors in your heart and blood vessels send a message to your brain to tell it what's going on, and your brain sends a message to make your heart beat slow down a bit—but it can't send messages below the site of your injury, so it can't regulate your blood pressure.'

'So what made it happen?' Kiki asked.

'Often it's a problem with your bladder that causes AD—you might have a urinary tract infection, which means your bladder's overfull,' Erin said. 'Would you mind if I examine you?'

'Sure,' Kiki said.

'Joe, I'd like you to keep monitoring Kiki's blood pressure, please, if that's OK,' Erin said.

'Yes, of course,' Joe said.

Erin examined her patient swiftly. As she'd expected, Kiki's skin was flushed and sweating above the level of her injury, but pale and with goose bumps below. But Kiki's bowel and bladder both appeared normal, with no distension.

'Your bowel and bladder both seem fine,' Erin said. 'I'd like to check out if you have any bruising or a pressure sore, because that might be a clue to what's irritating your system.'

'Sure,' Kiki said again.

There was no bruising evident—but as soon as Erin removed Kiki's socks she could see the problem. 'You've got an ingrown toenail,' she said.

'I have?' Kiki looked surprised.

'Whoever cuts your toenails for you has been

cutting the nail on your big toe a little bit too short, so the skin's folded over your nail and your nail's grown into the skin. I can see that it's red, swollen and tender just here. We can sort that out for you—we'll give you a little bit of local anaesthetic to numb your toe and cut away the edges of the nail, then put a chemical on the edge to stop that bit of the nail from growing back, so you won't get the problem again in future.'

'And that's what's made me feel this terrible and given me that pounding headache? Just an ingrown toenail?' Kiki looked shocked.

'Basically the pain receptors in your toe tried to send a signal to your brain, but it didn't get through and your nervous system reacted badly,' Erin explained.

'Can I get this again?' Kiki asked.

'It's very likely—as I said, the most common cause is if you have a water infection. I've got an information leaflet upstairs that I can give you, and it's a really good idea to keep a record of your blood pressure at home so you can show any medics what your normal baseline is.' Erin smiled at her. 'Once we've sorted out your toe, you'll be feeling better pretty quickly, but we'll keep a check on your blood pressure for a couple of hours before we let you go home again.'

'I'll get the local anaesthetic and sort out Kiki's toe,' Joe said.

'And I'll get you the leaflet,' Erin promised.

'So how was your AD patient?' Nate asked when Erin met him for lunch. 'Was it caused by a water infection?'

'Nope. Ingrown toenail,' Erin said. 'She's doing fine now. I've given her a leaflet about AD, and suggested she keeps a record of her blood pressure so if it happens again she can show the emergency team what's normal for her and flag up what the problem is so they know how to deal with it.'

'You know, it might be worth us doing a training session for the Emergency Department, covering a few of the complications they're likely to come across after our patients leave us,' Nate suggested.

'That's a good idea. We could go and talk to Nick about it.'

'Let's grab him before he goes into an afternoon meeting,' Nate said.

Nick was in his office when they went back onto the unit, so Erin knocked on his open door. 'Can we have a quick word?' she asked.

'I have a meeting in about fifteen minutes,' Nick said, 'so either it has to be really quick, or put something in my diary if you need a bit more time.'

'It'll be quick,' Nate said. 'Basically we want to do a training session with the Emergency Department, to give them an idea of the sort of complications they can come across with spinal patients after they've left us.'

'They had one of our old patients in with AD this morning,' Erin said, 'and we'd like to start with a session on that.'

'Are you talking about joint training sessions?' Nick asked.

'Yes,' Nate confirmed.

'It's good to see both sides of the team working together,' Nick said with a smile. 'By the way, Nate, I've seen your daughter's pieces about the sensory garden on both her school website and the hospital website. They're very good, but I was a bit surprised, given that the last time you discussed the sensory garden with Erin you seemed quite anti the idea.'

Nate laughed and said, 'I backed down. Let's say women can be persuasive—so, between Caitlin and Dr Leyton here, I didn't stand a chance.'

Erin punched his arm. 'Oh, come on, Nate. You admitted I was right. Or are you looking for another fight?'

'Yeah, yeah. Bring it on,' he teased. 'You missed me more times than you hit me in dodgeball.'

'Dodgeball?' Nick looked at them, his eyes narrowing. 'When did you play dodgeball together? Are you two—well, an item?'

'Absolutely not,' Erin said, at the same time as Nate said, 'You have to be kidding.'

Nick didn't look particularly convinced.

'My daughter came to live with me almost three months ago,' Nate said, 'and Erin here knows way more than I do about how a teenage girl's mind works. And she kindly offered to help when I was making a real mess of things—she took us to the trampoline park and ganged up on with me with Caitlin, playing dodgeball.'

'I was checking out the place to see if it would work as a venue for a team night out, at the same time,' Erin added. 'So everybody wins.'

'Hmm,' Nick said, but at least this time he sounded as if he believed them.

Erin and Nate exchanged a glance. Their first real slip-up. In future they'd need to be a lot more careful about how they acted towards each other on the ward, or the news of their relationship would leak out before they were ready.

'That was a near-miss in Nick's office,' Nate said when they met for breakfast on the Friday morning.

'We need to be careful,' Erin agreed. 'Maybe we should cool it a bit.'

'Too late,' he said, and reached across the table to hold her hand. 'You make me feel hot all over. Even just exchanging a glance with you makes my temperature spike.'

'You're thirty-five, not thirteen,' she reminded him with a grin.

He laughed. 'You missed your cue. You were meant to say that I make you feel hot all over, too.'

'You do,' she admitted.

Nate ate a forkful of his pancake and moaned.

'Was that me or the pancake?' she asked.

'Both.' He loaded his fork and leant across the table.

This felt *intimate*. But Erin let him feed her the forkful of pancake, then moaned in bliss.

'Was that me or the pancake?' He echoed her question.

'What do you think?' she teased.

He groaned. 'Play nice.'

'Both,' she said softly. 'I'm having pancakes next time. Cinnamon ones.' She waited a beat. 'But I'd prefer to share them with you somewhere else.'

'There's somewhere that makes better pancakes than this place?'

'Probably not quite as good. But the setting's more…intimate.'

His eyes went very dark. 'Are you suggesting what I think you're suggesting?'

'It involves wrought iron. And interesting lighting.'

He dragged in a breath. 'When Cait decides to visit Steph, we'll have a few days free.' He paused. 'We could have dinner. And breakfast.'

And in between, she thought; a shiver of pure desire slid down her spine. 'Half term?'

He shook his head. 'Cait already asked. Steph's too busy. Just as she's been too busy every weekend and school holiday since Cait came to live with me. I think she's scared that if Cait goes back to Devon, she'll refuse to come back to London.'

'Do you think that's likely?' Erin asked.

Nate thought about it. 'I hope not. I think she's settled with me. But I can't seem to make Steph see that every time she says she can't make a weekend or what have you, it makes Cait feel as if she's rejecting her.' He sighed. 'Given that I spent too many years putting my job before my daughter, I don't have room to criticise. And I don't want Cait feeling that I'm trying to get rid of her.'

'Then we'll take a rain check on the pancakes.

Maybe I can swap a shift or two during the holidays and we can do something fun together instead, to take her mind off it,' Erin said. 'Maybe we could do that locked room thing, and she could bring a friend.'

'That'd be nice,' Nate said. 'Are you sure you don't mind using your annual leave like that?'

'Of course I'm sure.' She squeezed his hand. 'And I get to spend time with you, too.'

'Not like this. Not just the two of us,' he said. 'I won't even be able to hold your hand.'

'That's OK. I can imagine it.' She moistened her lower lip. 'I have a good imagination.'

He groaned. 'And you've just put all sorts of pictures in my head. How am I supposed to spend the day being a sensible, level-headed surgeon when I want to pick you up and carry you off to some hidden corner and...'

'And?' she prompted. 'What happens next?'

He gave her a slow smile. 'Use your imagination.'

'And now you expect *me* to concentrate?'

'Sensible, level-headed neurologist. Yup.'

'We'll get our time together,' she said softly.

'We just have to be patient. And maybe waiting will be good for both of us.'

They managed to keep things professional at work, but snatched some time together whenever they could—meeting for breakfast on Fridays, and going to the park across the road from the hospital at lunchtime as many times as they thought they could get away with before anyone on the ward started commenting.

'I really want to dance with you,' Nate said one lunchtime. 'You and me in a little nightclub somewhere.'

'Which would mean asking your mum to babysit Caitlin—and what excuse are you going to give them for going out to some mysterious place with some mysterious person?' Erin asked. 'Because you can't say you've suddenly been called into Theatre, not if you're dressed up for a night out.'

'True,' Nate said with a sigh. 'And we're not ready to go public yet.'

They'd have to tell Caitlin, first; and this was still all so new. Plus part of Erin was scared that if they went public, it would be the first step to everything going wrong. 'Soon,' she said.

But Nate had a solution, the next time they walked in the park. He took a set of earphones from his pocket and plugged it into his phone. 'I've been thinking about it, and this is a night-club substitute,' he said with a smile. 'I'd much prefer this to be a dimly lit nightclub with a lit-tle jazz band playing at midnight, but the best I can do is midday, in the middle of these trees in the park, with music from my phone. One ear-phone each.'

Erin smiled. 'Very inventive, Mr Townsend.'

'Dance with me, Erin. I want to hold you,' he said softly, opening his arms.

She stepped forward, putting her arms round him, and let him put one of the earphones into her left ear. He put the other earphone into his right ear, then wrapped his arms round her.

'Close your eyes,' he said, 'and pretend we're on a real dance floor.'

She recognised the song as soon as the piano started playing; he'd picked one of the most ro-mantic songs she knew. And the lyrics brought tears to her eyes. Had he chosen it because it was a nice tune, or because he meant the words and wasn't quite sure how to say them to her?

Did he want to make her happy, and make her dreams come true?

Because she was pretty sure that was how she felt about him, too.

Still with her eyes closed, and her cheek pressed against his, she swayed with him to the music. And when he moved to kiss the corner of her mouth, she moved too so that he could kiss her properly—warm and sweet and poignant.

But then a passing teenager catcalled them.

And Erin remembered where they were: in the park opposite the hospital. Where anyone they knew could have gone for a lunchtime stroll and seen them.

She pulled away. 'I guess we'd better wait until it's a proper nightclub.'

'I guess,' Nate said, and his eyes were full of longing.

'Next time, the music ought to be "Somewhere" from *West Side Story*,' she said wryly.

He sang the first few bars of the song, and her

eyes widened. 'I didn't know you could sing that well. I'm impressed.'

'Don't be. I only know it because it was on a TV talent show programme and Cait loved it.'

She stroked his face. 'You still have a lovely voice. Don't do yourself down.'

'We'll get our somewhere. Some day,' he said.

'But for now we need to go back to work,' she said.

'And I can't even hold your hand across the park, because we'll be spotted and the hospital rumour mill will start.' He sighed. 'I guess we were lucky that it was teenagers who saw us dancing together, and not somebody from work.'

'This is hard,' Erin said. 'Half of me wants to go public. And half of me is scared it's going to go wrong.'

'Me, too,' he admitted. 'But Caitlin likes you.'

'As a friend. Being your girlfriend is a different thing,' she said. 'Especially given the way things are with her mum, right now. We can't rock the boat yet. Give it a little more time.'

'I know you're right,' he said. 'But I'm looking forward to our someday.'

'We just have to be inventive,' she said. 'Like your impromptu nightclub.'

Later in the week, Erin texted Nate.

How do you feel about some late-night cinema?

Love to, but I can't leave Cait on her own, he replied.

You don't have to. Welcome to the twenty-first century.

He called her. 'Explain.'

'We use technology,' she said. 'We can watch a film together, but we'll be in different houses.'

'Ah—using laptops,' he said, catching on quickly, 'so we're watching the same films.'

'And we can use video calling at the same time, so we can talk to each other during the film.'

'It isn't quite the same as sitting in the back row, holding hands,' he pointed out.

'Cinema substitute. Like your nightclub,' she said.

'Got you.'

They arranged to watch a film together at eleven p.m. that Sunday night.

'So, just to get this straight,' Nate said on screen, 'we're both sitting on the sofa and we're going to watch the same film.'

'Snuggled up with a throw,' Erin said. 'Which is the nearest we get to snuggling up with each other.'

'No throw, here. Would a cushion be an acceptable substitute?'

She laughed. 'Squishy in the middle? Yeah.'

Being warm and snuggly under a throw wasn't really a good substitute for curling up on the sofa together, but until they were ready to go public it was the best they could do.

'This is a bit like *Pillow Talk*,' Nate said.

'Hardly,' she scoffed. 'Apart from the fact we're not using a shared phone line and I know who you are instead of thinking you're this lovely, charming stranger, I'm not a repressed interior decorator. Plus you don't have a string of floozies—or do you?'

'No.' He groaned. 'Never argue films with someone who clearly had a misspent yout—'

He stopped abruptly, looking horrified. 'Sorry. I didn't mean that.'

'I know,' she said, equally softly. 'Actually, that's when I used to watch loads of films, day and night—and that was what got me through the worst bits. I wasn't picky about it; I just watched whatever was on satellite TV, so I saw everything from nineteen-thirties horror films through to musicals and action films.'

'I'm glad you had something to help.' He sighed. 'I wish I was with you right now, Erin. I really want to hold you.'

'Me, too—but at least we have video calling. If we'd been back in the fifties, with *Pillow Talk*, you're right—we would've been forced to use a party telephone line and all the neighbours would've been listening in to our conversation.'

'Yeah.'

'Now stop worrying about it and we'll watch the film together.'

It was an old one but it was one of Erin's favourite romcoms. She loved the scene where the hero declared himself at midnight on New Year's Eve, but it made her wonder: would she and Nate ever be able to declare how they felt to each other?

As if he'd picked up on her wistfulness, he said, 'Maybe we can snatch a day's annual leave and spend a day together—dating like normal people.'

'Sounds good,' she said.

'How does next Friday sound? So, instead of having breakfast before work, we actually get to go somewhere together?'

'Sounds perfect,' she said. 'Provided we can arrange the off-duty, it's a date.'

'Our first. Well, first proper date,' he amended.

And maybe one day they'd have a proper cinema date, holding hands in the back row. 'I'm looking forward to it,' she said. 'Night, Nate. Sweet dreams.'

'You, too,' he said, and blew her a kiss.

CHAPTER NINE

THE OFF-DUTY WORKED out just fine; so Nate and Erin had Friday off.

A whole day to spend together. Doing whatever they wanted. Far enough away from the hospital or anyone who knew them so they could hold hands and kiss in public without being spotted.

A normal date.

But, even though Nate had been longing for this, guilt nagged at him. He was supposed to be spending his time off with his daughter—and yet here he was, putting himself first.

Clearly the guilt showed in his face, because Erin raised an eyebrow when she saw him at the Tube™ station. 'Problem?'

'Not exactly,' he hedged.

'Spill,' she said.

The woman who didn't pull her punches. Who told things exactly like they were. Who expected the same from him. 'I feel pretty guilty about this,' he admitted.

'Because you ought to be saving your days off to spend with Caitlin?' she asked.

Typical Erin to get straight to the root of the problem. 'Yes.'

'Single parents are allowed to have a life of their own, too, you know. It's fine,' she said softly, and brushed her mouth against his.

Desire spun through him. Everything about this woman attracted him. Not just the way she looked: he liked her intelligence, her kindness, her calmness. And he was more than halfway to being head over heels in love with her. Not that he was going to tell her. It was still relatively early days, and he knew she had just as much emotional baggage to deal with as he did. The last thing he wanted to do was to scare her away by being too intense.

'I guess you're right,' he said instead.

She gave him a clenched-fist salute and a seriously sassy grin. 'Yes. The man admits it.'

He laughed, then, and tangled his fingers

through hers. 'Maybe we should think about telling Caitlin about us.'

'Do you think she'll be OK about it?'

'I don't know how she'll react,' he admitted. 'Though I do know she likes you. A lot,' he added. 'She's always talking about you. In a nice way.'

'I like her, too. A lot.'

He coughed.

She grinned. 'Are you fishing for compliments, Mr Townsend?'

'Yup. Shamelessly.'

She kissed him again. 'I like you, too. A lot.'

'Ditto.'

She narrowed her eyes at him. 'Not good enough.'

'I like you a lot,' he said. 'More than I've liked anyone for a very long time.'

'Ditto,' she said.

'If I said to you that that wasn't good enough, you'd just laugh at me.'

'Yup.' She smiled. 'Stop worrying, Nate. And let's wait a little longer before we tell Caitlin. Let's think about the best way to tell her so she knows that, whatever happens between you and me, you'll always love her and she'll always be friends with me.'

'Yes. It's finding the right words that's the problem.'

'They'll be there when the time's right,' she said. 'That's one of Rachel's sayings.'

'Along with "Never trouble trouble, till trouble troubles you",' he said. 'I remember you telling me once.' He drew her closer to him. 'I can't believe we're actually going on a proper date.'

'Are you saying our breakfasts and our sneaky walks in the park at lunchtime and our cinema session using video calling weren't proper dates?' she teased.

He laughed. 'You know what I mean. We're actually doing something that normal couples do.'

'We're doing OK,' she said. 'Unconventional's working for us.'

'True.'

They headed for the British Museum where he'd booked tickets for the exhibition they both wanted to see, and wandered hand in hand round the displays.

'Oh, I love this. It's like a boar's head,' Erin said, stopping by one case. She read the display notes quickly. 'It's a carnyx—an ancient war-horn from Scotland, used to terrify their enemies. And look—you can listen to someone playing a replica.' She picked up the headphones and pressed the buttons. 'Yep. I think this would scare me, hearing this booming across the glens.'

Nate didn't think that anything would scare Erin. She faced things head-on. But he dutifully listened to the recording of the carnyx.

Erin was delighted by the intricate patterns in the shields and the stonework. When they wandered over to the display of golden torcs, he looked at her. 'I can imagine you wearing one of those. A Celtic warrior queen.'

'Shouldn't a Celtic warrior queen have red hair?'

'Yours is the colour of ripe corn—and I love these wild curls.' He twined the end of one soft curl round his finger. 'I understand why you have to wear it tied back at work, but I'd love to see your hair loose some time.'

She wrinkled her nose. 'It's not great, you know. It just goes mad and frizzy.'

He wanted to make the rest of her feel mad and frizzy, too—but he knew he needed to take things at her pace. 'You'd still look beautiful wearing one of these torcs. Wise and regal, then.'

She bowed her head in acknowledgement. 'Why, thank you.'

When they reached the end of the exhibition, she took him in search of the Lewis Chessmen. 'I've always loved these. Mikey bought me a full-sized replica set for my twenty-first birthday.'

'I didn't know you played chess.'

'I learned after Mikey's accident. It helped both of us, I think.'

'Your brother sounds like an amazing guy.'

'He is.' She paused. 'Maybe you could meet him some time.'

'Have you told him about me?'

She nodded.

'And?'

'He likes the sound of you—but he also knows you're not going to meet him and Louisa, his fiancée, until I'm ready.'

Was she ready to introduce him to her closest family? Nate wondered. And he hadn't asked Erin to meet anyone in his family other than Caitlin. Maybe it was time to introduce her to his mother—though he was pretty sure that Sara had worked out the situation for herself already.

As if Erin guessed what he was thinking, she said softly, 'I don't think we're quite ready to go public yet.'

Maybe she was right. They still didn't have the right words.

'Let's go and have lunch,' she suggested.

'Good idea.' He let her switch the subject and chatter about museums while they ate, and he was about to order coffee when she said, 'How about coffee at my place?'

'I'd like that. Thanks.'

They walked hand in hand from the Tube™ station back to Erin's flat. When she'd made coffee, she sat down next to him on the sofa and Nate scooped her onto his lap. 'Is this OK?' he checked, wanting to be close to her but wanting to keep things at a pace where she was comfortable.

'Very OK.' She smiled and kissed him.

The touch of her mouth against his made him feel as if all his senses had gone into overdrive. He wrapped his arms round her and kissed her back; but when he broke the kiss, he realised that his hands had slid underneath the hem of her top. Too much, too soon.

'Sorry.' He moved his hands away, even though he missed the warmth and smoothness of her skin against his palms.

She stroked his face. 'I wasn't saying no, Nate.'

He went very still. Was she suggesting…?

'But you're right about something,' she continued. 'My sofa isn't a good place to do this.'

No, he was definitely jumping the gun. Clearly she wanted him to stop.

He was about to scoop her back off his lap when she said quietly, 'Maybe we need to move to my bedroom.'

He stared at her, his heart pounding. 'Are you saying…?'

She nodded.

'Are you sure about this?' he checked.

'I'm sure.' Her eyes looked huge and full of sincerity. 'Completely sure.'

'But—' His throat dried. 'I don't have any protection with me.'

'I do.'

His surprise must have shown on his face because she said, 'I bought condoms last night.'

So she'd planned this? For a moment, he couldn't breathe. Couldn't think straight. Then he kissed her, very gently. 'Just so you know,' he said, 'if you change your mind at any point, that's totally fine. If you need me to stop at any point, even if you think it's too late, just tell me and I'll stop immediately.'

Her eyes filmed with tears. 'Thank you. I know you're not Andrew and I trust you. But it's nice that you…' Her breath caught. 'That you understand.'

'I do. And you have no idea how good it makes me feel that you trust me. Just as I trust you.' He wanted to say a different word there, but he didn't want to push her. To rush her. To scare her away. 'Make love with me, Erin.'

'What a very good idea, Mr Townsend.' She

slid off his lap and he stood up, letting her lead him to her room.

The walls were cream, the curtains were burgundy—but best of all was the wide double bed with fairy lights wound round the wrought-iron frame.

'Now I know what you meant about interesting lighting. That's *so* girly,' he said with a grin.

'Funny you should say that, with me being a girl.'

'You're not a girl,' he corrected. 'You're all woman. And you're gorgeous, inside and out.'

She blushed. 'Nice line.'

'No line. It's how I feel.' His gaze held hers. 'I already told you, I like you a lot.'

'Ditto.'

'And any time you need me to stop,' he repeated, 'we stop.'

'No stopping,' she said, went over to the window and closed the curtains. Then she switched on the fairy lights. 'Still think they're girly?'

'Yup. But they're sexy, too.' He waited a beat. 'Like you.'

'Well, hey.' She brushed her mouth against his, then undid the top button of his shirt.

Then he realised that her fingers were actually shaking.

He drew her hands to his mouth and kissed her fingers. 'You OK?'

'Nervous,' she admitted.

'Me, too.' He kissed the tip of her nose. 'But this is you and me. It's going to be just fine.'

For a moment, she looked unsure. But then she lifted her chin and finished unbuttoning his shirt. She tugged the soft cotton free from the waistband of his trousers, then slid the garment from his shoulders. 'Nice pecs, Mr Townsend.'

'Why, thank you, Dr Leyton. I value your personal opinion as much as your professional opinion.' He held her gaze. 'My turn?'

'I think so.' She lifted her arms to make it easier for him to remove her top.

He drew the tip of his forefinger around the lacy outline of her bra. 'Your skin's so soft, Erin.' And touching wasn't enough. He dipped his head and kissed all along the line of her collarbone.

When she caught her breath, he held back again. 'OK?' he checked.

'Very OK,' she said. Her voice was shaky, and he really wasn't sure about this until she added, 'I'm kind of looking forward to those clever surgeon's hands touching me.'

'Oh, are you, now?' He stole another kiss, and removed her bra one-handedly. 'Clever enough for you?'

'Showing off, a tad,' she said, and removed his trousers.

The touch of her fingers against his skin sent desire lancing through him. 'How about this?' he asked, and removed her jeans, stroking every centimetre of skin he uncovered.

'Better,' she said, and he was gratified to hear the huskiness in her voice.

He kissed her lightly. 'Protection,' he said. 'And then I'm all yours. Do what you will with me.'

She took a packet of condoms from her bedside drawer and handed it to him.

'I think,' he said, 'I'd like to see how clever those neurologist's hands of yours are.'

'Hmm,' she said. 'That sounds like a challenge.'

'It is.'

He wasn't sure which of them removed the last bits of each other's clothing, but then he'd pushed her duvet aside and was lying against her pillows, and she was kneeling beside him.

He took a condom from the packet and handed it to her. 'You're in control,' he said, and grasped the wrought-iron headboard between the fairy lights.

She brushed her mouth against his. 'Thank you. For understanding.'

'Any time.' And how he loved her for being brave enough to get past the vulnerability. For being brave enough to trust him.

She ripped open the foil packet and eased the condom over his penis. And then she straddled him. When she slid her hand round his shaft and positioned him against her entrance, he had to grip the headboard that little bit more tightly. And then slowly, gently, she lowered herself onto him.

He desperately wanted to wrap his arms round her and hold her close, but he needed her to trust him completely. So he lay still, letting her set the pace. And he was rewarded by seeing the confidence grow in her face as she moved over him.

Just as he felt his climax starting to bubble through him, she peeled his fingers off the headboard; in response, he sat up and wrapped his arms round her, pushing deep into her at the same time.

She jammed her mouth over his, and he felt her body surge against his, pushing him into his own climax.

And he'd never, ever had such a feeling of sweetness before.

After he'd dealt with the condom, he climbed back into bed beside her, wrapped her in his arms and pulled the duvet over them.

'Erin. I lo—'

Before he could finish the sentence, she pressed her forefinger against his lips. 'Don't say it, Nate.'

Because she didn't feel the same, and she didn't want to let him down by admitting it?

As if she guessed what he was thinking, she said, 'Because it's too soon, not because I don't feel the same way about you. Those particular words…I don't really trust them.'

The shadow of her ex. Again.

And it would take time before he could melt that particular shadow away. He needed to take it slowly. 'OK. I understand,' he said.

'For now, let's just be,' she said.

It felt good, lying there with her in his arms. Nothing to think about or worry about except each other.

Though he couldn't help noticing the time.

'Erin. I really don't want to go, but I need to pick Caitlin up—'

'I know. It's OK.'

'One day,' he said softly, 'we'll get to spend the night together.'

She chuckled. 'I'm glad you're a better surgeon than you are when it comes to words. Day and night are two separate things, you know.'

'They won't be,' he said. 'Because I intend to make you lose track of time.'

'I'll take that as a promise,' she said, and kissed him lightly. 'You'd better go, or you'll get stuck in traffic. But thank you for today. For—well, being understanding.'

Which told him that either the men she'd dated

since her ex hadn't been understanding, or she hadn't trusted them enough to get as far as telling them what had happened to her. 'Thank *you*,' he said. 'For trusting me.'

'I'm older and wiser and a better judge of character, now,' she said. 'And I like you, Nate Townsend. I like you a whole lot.'

And one day, he hoped, she'd let herself love him.

He climbed out of bed and started to get dressed. When she sat up, he shook his head. 'Stay there. You look comfortable. And cute.'

'But—'

'I can see myself out,' he said. 'And I guess I'll see you tomorrow.'

'You can count on that.'

He finished dressing, then gave her a lingering kiss goodbye. 'One day,' he said softly. 'Keep that in mind.'

'I will,' she promised.

CHAPTER TEN

ERIN LAY CURLED in her bed, all warm and cosy and totally replete.

Nate had been a considerate lover, and she really appreciated the fact that he'd been so careful with her. She had a pretty good idea how he felt about her, now—though she'd stopped him saying it out loud, because the words scared her stupid. In her experience, love didn't work out, and she really wanted this to work out. Nate was important to her and so was Caitlin.

But what if it all went wrong, the way it usually did for her relationships? It wasn't just her feelings at stake any more. Maybe she should back off before everyone ended up hurt…

On Monday morning, Erin was busy in clinic. 'So tell me about your symptoms,' she said to the worried-looking woman in front of her.

'I've been getting these weird feelings in my neck for the last couple of weeks,' Harriet said. 'It's kind of like jerking—I can't stop it happening. I saw my doctor and he said I'd probably just slept awkwardly and it would go away, but it's got worse over the last two weeks so he sent me here.'

Erin had already seen from the notes that Harriet had no previous significant medical history and wasn't on any medication. 'Does anyone in your family have a history of neurological illness?' she asked. 'Anything like epilepsy?'

'Not that I know of,' Harriet said. 'Is that what I've got?'

'I'll need to examine you properly before I can give you a diagnosis,' Erin said, 'so I'm afraid I have a few more questions. Is there any pattern to the movements? Do they stop or get better when you're relaxed? And do you know if you get them in your sleep?'

'There's no real pattern—they just start and I have no idea when it's going to happen or how long it'll go on. Though they seem a bit worse when I'm stressed,' Harriet said, 'which is probably why they're getting more frequent. I get them in my sleep, too. My boyfriend's the one who noticed it first. It woke him up.'

Erin had to damp down the little flare of envy. What would it be like, to wake up in your boyfriend's arms? It was something she'd never done, something she'd never allowed herself to do, because she'd always compartmentalised her relationships.

Would Nate be the one she finally woke up to?

'I'm really scared that there's something really wrong with me,' Harriet said. Then she grimaced. 'Oh, no. It's starting again.'

Erin could see immediately that the muscles in the nape of Harriet's neck were jerking rhythmically, on both sides.

'I'm going to do a full neurological examination,' Erin said, 'and then I'm going to run some tests to find out what's causing the twitching—it's something called myoclonus, which basically means that your muscles contract and relax. It's the same sort of thing as hiccups or if you're dropping off to sleep and suddenly feel a "start", though it's rarer for the muscles in your neck to be affected.'

'Is it serious? Am I going to die?' Harriet asked. 'Is it catching?'

'It's not catching and it's not fatal,' Erin reassured her, 'and actually your doctor was right because with some people it does just disappear.'

'So what causes it?'

'Epilepsy, which is why I asked you if anyone in your family had it,' Erin explained, 'or an infection. Sometimes it happens if someone has a spinal injury or a brain injury—and sometimes it just happens and we don't know why.'

'I haven't had any accidents or banged into anything,' Harriet said. 'So it can't be a brain injury, and my back's fine. And I haven't had any kind of bug.'

'OK. Let me examine you and we'll take it from there,' Erin said. 'I might need to run quite a few tests, and there will be a bit of waiting around, so are you OK to be here all day? Do you want me to call anyone to come and keep you company? Your boyfriend?'

'No. I'll be OK,' Harriet said.

There was nothing unusual in the neurological exam; a routine electroencephalograph, blood tests and an MRI scan all came back clear, too.

'So far, I can't find a physical cause, so I'm going to give you a needle EMG,' Erin said. 'That stands for an electromyograph. What it means is that I put a needle into your muscles—it sounds much scarier than it is, and it doesn't hurt—and it records the electrical activity of your muscles and plots everything for me on a graph so I can analyse it. I normally use an EMG to help me diagnose the cause of pain in the back or the neck, or to show if there's a nerve compression injury, such as carpal tunnel syndrome.'

But the EMG was clear, too.

'So the good thing is that there isn't a physical injury,' Erin said. 'What I'm going to do is give you some anti-epilepsy medication, and ask you to come back and see me in a fortnight to see how you're getting on. I'm pretty sure the medication will stop the muscle contractions, but if it doesn't then I can try a couple of other treatments. The most important thing is that you don't worry.' She smiled at Harriet. 'Which I know is easier said than done. But you can call me here at any time, and if it gets worse instead of better then come back before your appointment and we'll try something else.'

Over the next couple of weeks, Nate and Erin managed to snatch time together around their shifts, and sneaked in a half day where Nate whisked her back to his house for lunch in bed.

'I'm sure people are going to start to guess about us at work,' he said. 'I have a goofy smile on my face every time I look at you.'

'Me, too,' she said. 'You know you said you wanted to make me feel like a teenager? Mission accomplished.'

'The way I feel about you—I know, I know, you don't want me to say the words. But I never expected to feel like this about anyone again.' He stroked her face. 'Maybe it's time we went public.'

'We need to tell Caitlin, first,' Erin said. 'If she's OK with it, then we'll go public.'

'So when are we going to tell her?'

'Saturday?' Erin suggested.

'Saturday,' he agreed. 'And we'll plan our strategy over breakfast on Friday.'

'Sounds perfect,' she said.

On Thursday evening, Nate's phone pinged with a text.

'I'll get that for you, Dad,' Caitlin said, before he could tell her that it was fine and to leave it.

She picked up the phone, and because the message was short it was fully visible on the front of his lock screen. 'It's from Erin—she says see you at breakfast.' She paused. 'And there's a kiss.' She stared at him, and was it his own guilty conscience or was there a note of accusation in her voice when she asked, 'Why are you seeing Erin for breakfast?'

'To discuss a patient,' he said swiftly.

'But you'd do that at work, not at home.' She frowned. 'I was talking to Shelby at school about you and she thought Erin was your girlfriend. I said she wasn't, but *are* you dating Erin?'

Stalling for time, he asked, 'Why would I be dating her?'

'Are you seeing her secretly?' Caitlin demanded.

'Because otherwise why would she text you with a kiss on the end?'

Oh, hell. Clearly his expression had confirmed her worst fears because then Caitlin shook her head, looking hurt and miserable. 'When you and Erin took me to Kew and that locked room place, it wasn't because you wanted to be with me, was it? You just used me as an excuse to date Erin in secret.'

He could definitely tell her that wasn't true. Of course he'd wanted to spend time with his daughter. 'That's not true, Cait, I—'

But it was too late. She was already running upstairs and he heard her bedroom door slam. His heart sinking, he realised that they'd gone right back to how things had been when Caitlin had first come to live with him. He'd just managed to ruin all the progress they'd made.

This was a row he couldn't handle on his own. Caitlin wouldn't believe anything he said. It was way past the time of telling her the truth—and he needed to do that with Erin at his side. Just as they'd originally planned to do.

He grabbed his phone and called her. 'Erin,

we've got a problem. Caitlin picked up your text and she's worked everything out for herself. Except she thinks I used her to date you in secret—and she didn't believe me when I said that's not true. I know it's a lot to ask, but could you maybe come over and help me talk to her?'

'Of course I will.' Erin's voice was calm and reassuring, and Nate realised then how much he was panicking. Which was ridiculous. At work, he performed operations that carried a high risk of paralysis for his patients and he was cool, calm and in absolute control. Why couldn't he be like that at home with his daughter?

'Even if she's upset and angry, she might listen to me because she knows I've been in her shoes,' Erin continued. 'I'm on my way now. Go and talk to her—even if it's through a closed door and she doesn't answer you. It'll reassure her that you care.'

He didn't have a clue what to say but he'd wing it. There was no other choice. 'Thanks.'

When he ended the call, he went upstairs and knocked on Caitlin's door. There was no answer, as he'd half expected. But at least she wasn't blasting out music, so she'd be able to hear whatever he said. He took a deep breath. All he could tell her was the truth and open his heart to her.

'Cait, I admit, I am dating Erin, but it's not why I asked her to come out with us. We really were just friends at the beginning, but I've come to see her as more than a friend over the last few weeks. And when I've taken her out with you it's because I want to do things with *you*, Cait—to do things with you as a family.'

She didn't answer.

He tried again. 'I love you. Yes, I know it was tough when you first came to live with me, and we've both had to make a few adjustments, but I thought we were getting along pretty well.'

There was still no answer.

He battled on grimly, telling her how important she was to him. Even though he didn't think the message was getting through, he had to try.

Finally, to his relief, the doorbell went. It had to be Erin. He went downstairs to let her in, and then she followed him up to Caitlin's room.

When Erin knocked on the door, there was still no answer.

'Caitlin, it's Erin. I'm coming in because we need to talk and sort this out, OK?' Erin said.

When Caitlin still said nothing, Erin opened the door. But, to Nate's shock, his daughter's room was empty.

'Oh, my God—no wonder she didn't answer us. She's not here.' He dragged in a breath. 'She can't have run away. She *can't*. And when could she have left the house? I was right here outside her door all the time...' He closed his eyes. 'Except when I rang you. She must have gone out then, and I didn't hear the front door.'

He dragged his phone from his pocket and called Caitlin's mobile. 'Switched off,' he reported grimly.

'OK. Let's think logically. Where's she likely to have gone?' Erin asked. 'The back garden? Didn't you say you were giving her a patch of her own there?'

But the back garden was empty, too.

'She might have gone to my mum's. Or maybe her friend Shelby's.' He called both homes, with the same result: Caitlin wasn't there, but if they heard anything from her they'd call Nate immediately.

'She wouldn't have gone back to Devon,' Nate said, 'because she doesn't have the money for a train ticket.'

'Maybe she called her mum,' Erin suggested. 'Steph could've bought her a ticket to pick up at the station.'

It wasn't a call he relished, but if it meant his daughter would be safe he would've walked a mile across burning coals. He rang Stephanie. 'It's Nate. Just a quick question—has Caitlin called you at all this evening?'

'No. Why—what's happened?' she asked.

'We had a bit of a fight,' Nate admitted.

He could almost see her shrug when she said, 'She'll get over it.'

How could Steph be so matter-of-fact about it? Didn't it tie her up in knots when she fell out with their daughter? 'Uh-huh,' he said, trying to sound noncommittal.

Her voice sharpened with suspicion. 'What aren't you telling me, Nate?'

He owed it to her to tell her the truth. Plus if

Caitlin did ring, Stephanie could maybe find out where she was and call him to let him know so he could go and fetch her. 'Don't panic, but she's not actually here at the moment. I'm trying to work out where she's gone. I wondered if she'd called you and asked you to buy her a train ticket to Devon.'

'Oh, my God—you're telling me you've lost my daughter?' Stephanie's voice rose to a shriek.

'She's my daughter, too,' Nate pointed out, 'and right now I'm trying to find her. Look, if she calls you, please just keep her talking and let me know where she is so I can go and get her. Meanwhile I'll keep looking for her—and I promise I'll call you the second I've found her.'

'Maybe she's gone to the sensory garden,' Erin suggested when he ended the call. 'It's somewhere she loves and she can be on her own to think things through. That's what I'd do in her shoes.'

'OK. Let's go.'

'Wait—we can check from here.' She called Ayesha, the chair of the Friends of the London Victoria, who organised the rota. 'Hi, Ayesha, it's Erin from the spinal unit. I was just wondering—who's working at the sensory garden this evening?' She explained the situation swiftly. 'Can you do me a huge favour and contact Nola for me and ask her if she can check if Caitlin's there, then call me to let me know either way? Thanks so much. I really appreciate it.'

To Nate's mounting dismay, when Ayesha called Erin back it was to report that there was no sign of Caitlin at the sensory garden.

'Ayesha gave my number to Nola, and Nola's going to call me straight away if Caitlin turns up there,' Erin told him. 'OK. Green spaces. Where's the nearest garden to here?'

'There's a park on the corner,' Nate said.

'Let's try there.'

There were little groups of teenagers scattered about the park, but Caitlin wasn't among them.

'OK. I'm out of places where she could've gone. Time to call the police,' Nate said. He'd just found the number of the local station when Erin's phone shrilled.

'Hello? Yes, Nola? She's—oh, thank God.'

Nate closed his eyes for a moment, grateful beyond belief that his silent prayers had been answered.

'Thank you. Yes, we will.' Erin ended the call. 'She's at the sensory garden,' she said. 'Nola's giving her a mug of hot chocolate and keeping her there until we get there. I said we'd go and fetch her now.'

Nate drove as fast as he could to the hospital, inwardly cursing the heavy traffic. But at least he knew his daughter was safe. That was the main thing. Once he'd got her back, he was never letting her go again.

Nate was silent on the drive to the hospital, and Erin noticed that his fingers were white where he was gripping the steering wheel so hard.

He'd obviously just had one of the worst scares of his life, thinking that his daughter had gone missing.

And it was all her fault.

If she hadn't sent that stupid text, Caitlin wouldn't have picked it up and gone into a meltdown.

And the fact that Caitlin's reaction to the idea of

them dating was to run away told her that the girl was really panicking about it. Given that Caitlin had been sent to live with her dad after her mum remarried, the girl was clearly worrying that Nate was going to abandon her, too, and she'd have to start all over again somewhere else.

What Erin had kept from Nate was that Nola had said that Caitlin had started uprooting plants in the sensory garden. To Erin, it was a clear signal that Caitlin wasn't ready to consider even the idea of Nate and Erin dating, because she'd gone straight to the place that had brought them together in the first place and started destroying it.

And it was a sharp reminder of what she'd believed for years—that love didn't work out. Her own relationships had always gone wrong. It hadn't worked out for Nate and Steph, either, and the situation with Caitlin now was the fallout from that.

Nate was a good man. He was doing his best for his daughter. But he hadn't been able to make it work with Caitlin's mother. With Erin's track record, what chance did they stand? And if she let him get any closer—or let Caitlin get any closer—when it went wrong that would be three lives shattered.

So there was only one thing Erin could do, even though this was going to break her heart, and that was to call things off between her and Nate. Walk away.

When he parked the car, she touched his hand.

'Nate, I think you need to talk to her on your own and reassure her that she comes first.'

He frowned. 'It'd be better if she hears it from both of us.'

'There can't be an us,' she said softly. 'Not any more. It's over.'

He stared at her, looking totally shocked. 'Erin, no.'

'There is no other way,' she said. 'You're important to me, Nate, and in another life I really would've wanted to make a life with you, but it's not going to work out between us. I've already made someone pay a high price for my selfishness and I'm not going to do that again. Remember, I've been where Caitlin is. I understand how she feels. And right now she needs you to put her first. So go and see your daughter, show her how much you love her and it'll be OK. But from now on you and I can only be colleagues.'

Saying the words was easy. The hard bit was trying not to let it show that it was ripping her heart out. 'Good luck. I hope it all goes OK.' And she got out of Nate's car and walked away before she started crying and gave herself away.

CHAPTER ELEVEN

ERIN WAS ENDING it between them?

But—but…

Feeling more helpless than he'd ever done in his life, Nate watched her walk away, her steps sure and swift. His first instinct was to go after her; and yet they were here because Caitlin had run away. Right now, his daughter needed his full attention. And, no matter how much he wanted to be, he couldn't physically be in two places at the same time.

The realisation sickened him: he'd been deluding himself all along in thinking that he could have it all. He had to choose between his daughter and the woman he loved, after all. Steph had chosen her relationship over their daughter, and if he did the same then Caitlin would be completely alone. Nate also knew that Erin had been in Caitlin's shoes, so she understood exactly how the teenager felt and had done the right thing. He needed to follow Erin's example and do the same. Even though it was ripping him in two.

Grimly, he walked into the sensory garden area. Several people he recognised were working on the raised beds; they looked up as he came over.

'Caitlin's with Nola in the potting shed,' one of them said.

'Thanks—Mindy, isn't it?'

She nodded. 'I'm afraid Caitlin's been uprooting most of the plants in the bed she's been working on.'

The area she'd spent hours working on over the last few weeks? And she'd just trashed it? Nate stared at Mindy in disbelief. 'But she loves the garden! Oh, no. I'm so sorry.' He rubbed a hand across his face. 'Look, I'll pay for the replacement plants and what have you.'

'She was pretty upset. And she could've done a lot worse,' Mindy said sympathetically.

'Even so, this isn't like her. And I'm really sorry.'

'I know this isn't like her. She's a good kid,' Mindy said. 'We all think a lot of her. It'll sort itself out.' She patted his arm. 'I think right now she needs her dad.'

And her dad needed to put her first instead of focusing on his own selfish feelings. Yeah. He got that. 'The potting shed, you said? Thanks.'

Caitlin was silent and white-faced when he knocked on the door of the potting shed.

'She's quite safe,' Nola said.

'Thank you for looking after her,' Nate said. Though he knew there was an awful lot of damage to repair—and not just to the garden. 'I talked to Mindy. We'll sort everything out.'

'Absolutely,' Nola said, and to his relief she was tactful enough to leave them alone.

'Ready to go?' he asked Caitlin.

She refused to talk to him.

'OK. Let me give this to you straight,' he said. 'Ready or not, we're going home. It's up to you if you want to finish your hot chocolate first, but we're going home. Together. End of discussion.'

Again, Caitlin said nothing, but she put her mug down. Then she walked to the car with him in silence. He sent a quick text to all the people he'd called about Caitlin, saying that he'd found her and she was fine; he'd be in touch later but needed a serious talk with her first. Then he drove them home. Caitlin kept her face turned away throughout the whole journey, and as soon as they were inside the house she ran upstairs and slammed her door.

Last time he'd made the mistake of leaving her be. He'd learned from that, so this time he went straight after her, opened the door and went to sit on her bed.

'Go away,' she said through clenched teeth.

He could see that she was close to tears. 'I'm not going anywhere. I'm your dad, I love you and we need to talk,' he said.

She stared at him. 'But you hate me, and I've messed everything up.'

'I don't hate you. Far from it. I was worried sick when I realised you'd gone. And you haven't messed everything up. You made a mistake, yes, but that's what life's about,' Nate said. 'Nobody's perfect and nobody gets everything right all the time. The important thing is to admit that you're wrong, apologise, learn from your mistake and then do what you can to put it right.'

'But I ruined the garden—they'll never let me back there now,' she said miserably.

'Caitlin, you uprooted a few plants and it was only in the patch you'd worked on. You damaged your own work, yes, but nobody else's. You can explain that you were upset and you're sorry and you'd like to make amends. Tell them you'll pay for the damaged plants from your pocket money and you'll go on the rota to do your least favourite job for the next month.'

'They won't have me back,' Caitlin repeated.

'Yes, they will. They like you and they know this kind of behaviour isn't normal for you.'

She stared at him. 'And you don't hate me?'

'Not even slightly. I love you,' he repeated.

Her eyes narrowed. 'But you left me when I was little, so how do I know you really mean it now?'

He sighed. 'Your mum and I were very young when we had you. I'm not making excuses or blaming anyone, because your mum and I both made mistakes and we should both have done things differently. When you were born, I was still a student and then a junior doctor, so I worked really long hours and I was too tired to help your mum as much as she needed. Maybe I should've given up my dream of being a spinal surgeon and worked in a different area of the hospital instead, but I didn't—and that was my fault.'

'But if you hadn't trained as a spinal surgeon then you wouldn't have been able to fix that man's back.'

'No,' he admitted. 'Though someone else would've done it.'

'So you're saying you chose your job over me.'

'I wanted everything,' Nate said. Just as he did now. 'But it didn't work out that way.' Just as it wasn't going to work out now. But this time Caitlin wasn't going to be the one who paid the price. 'I can't change the past, but I have learned from it—and that's why I'm here for you now and I always will be.' He took her hand. 'I'm not going to abandon you, Caitlin. You're my daughter and you live with me now, and nothing's going to change that—least of all a few uprooted plants.'

'But how do I know?'

'That I'm telling you the truth?' He took his

wallet from his pocket and handed it to her. 'Look in the flap.'

She did, and saw the photograph of herself as a toddler sitting on his shoulders. 'That's you? But you're so young! And the photograph…it's a bit creased.'

'It's a very old photo,' he agreed. 'And it's creased because it's had to fit in every wallet I've owned over the last eleven years. It's my favourite photograph of you. I've got others—lots of others—but this one's special. Now look on the other side.'

It was a much more recent photo of them together in the Sky Garden. They were smiling, with their arms wrapped round each other.

'Erin took that.'

'Yeah.' Erin. He still couldn't believe she'd gone.

Caitlin bit her lip. 'She's going to hate me for this.'

'Erin's been in your shoes, remember. She's going to understand.'

'But it's her garden and I wrecked it.'

'You uprooted a few plants and that can be

fixed,' he repeated. 'You and Erin get on well and what you did tonight isn't going to change that.' Though it had changed something else: Erin had ended their romance. She'd walked away to let him salvage his relationship with his daughter.

'Does she know I—well…?' Caitlin bit her lip again.

'Ran away? Yes. And she knows about the garden.'

Caitlin looked worried. 'And she's not here now.'

'She's busy,' Nate fibbed. 'I'm sure she'll speak to you later. But whatever happens you're my daughter, I love you and nothing will ever change that.'

'You were dating Georgina when I came to live with you, and you broke up with her because of me,' Caitlin pointed out.

'Georgina and I weren't getting on that well before you came to London, believe me. We would've split up anyway, so that wasn't because of you,' he reassured her.

'Are you and Erin going to split up because of me?'

They already had, but he wasn't going to make

Caitlin feel guilty. 'I thought you weren't happy about me seeing Erin?'

'I wasn't. Because when I found out you were seeing her, I thought you'd choose her over me, the way Mum chose Craig over me, and I was scared about where I'd have to go next.'

'You're not going anywhere. You live with me. And the only reason we didn't tell you we were dating was because we didn't want to worry you—we were trying to protect you in case things didn't work out between us and we didn't want you getting hurt, but we got it very wrong and I'm sorry for that. I can't answer for your mum,' Nate said gently, 'but sometimes we get into a complicated situation and can't see an easy way out. Your mum loves you, too.'

'It doesn't feel like it.'

'Relationships aren't always easy,' Nate said. He made a mental note to ring Stephanie and get her to tell their daughter that she loved her. 'And love stretches. Just because you love one person, it doesn't mean you can't love anyone else. Otherwise people wouldn't have more than one child, would they?'

'You and Mum only had me.'

'Circumstances,' he said. 'If we'd stayed together—and maybe if I'd had a different job—you might've had a brother or a sister. Maybe one of each.'

'So you and Erin—you're not going to split up because of what I did?'

'Erin's been where you are,' he said. 'She'd never put you through that by making me choose between you.'

A tear trickled down her face as she worked it out for herself. 'You mean she walked away instead, so you didn't have to choose?'

'It's OK,' Nate said. Even though it wasn't and there was a massive Erin-shaped hole where his heart should've been.

'No, it's *not* OK. You have to talk to her. Make her change her mind,' Caitlin said, her face desperate. 'Make her come back. Fix this, the way you fix people's backs.'

Spinal surgery was an awful lot less complicated than fixing relationships, he thought. And Erin came with complications that Caitlin didn't know about; she'd admitted that she never usually let people get close, so had she seized on Caitlin's reaction as an excuse not to let him and Caitlin close?

'Sometimes life doesn't work out the way you want it to,' he said gently.

'But if you talk to her...' Caitlin pleaded.

He could talk to Erin until he was blue in the face, but he still wasn't sure if he could change her mind.

'I wouldn't mind if you did end up getting married to Erin—she's a lot nicer than Craig.'

He smiled and ruffled her hair. 'Right.'

'Talk to her, Dad. Fix it. I'll do—I'll clean the bathroom for the next month.'

Nate had to hide a smile. She'd been listening, then, when he'd suggested that she put her name down at the sensory garden for the chore she hated most, and she was offering to do the same at home.

'OK. I'll talk to her. Tomorrow.'

'Talk to her *now*,' Caitlin said.

He shook his head. 'I'm not leaving you on your own.'

'I'm not going to run away again, Dad. I know that was stupid.'

He hugged her. 'I know you won't run away again, but you're upset and I don't want to leave you on your own.'

'Can I go and stay with Gran, then?' She bit her lip. 'Does Gran know I ran away?'

He nodded. 'So does your mother. And Shelby's mum.'

'Everyone knows?' she whispered, looking miserable and embarrassed.

'And everyone understands,' he said. 'Everyone will have forgotten about it by Monday.'

'Does Gran hate me?'

'Nobody hates you,' he reassured her. 'Here. Let her tell you herself. Call her.' He took his phone from his pocket and handed it over. And he sat with his arms round his daughter while she talked to her grandmother.

'Gran says she'll come over,' Caitlin informed him when she'd ended the call. 'So now you can ring Erin.'

'She might be out.'

She gave him a speaking look, then took her own phone from her pocket and called a number.

'Erin? It's Caitlin. I want to say sorry. I messed things up and I got everything wrong. I don't really know what to say to make things right, but I know you're important to Dad—and you're important to me, too,' she said.

There was a pause; Erin was clearly speaking, but Nate couldn't hear any of the words.

'Uh-huh,' Caitlin said.

Another pause, with more he couldn't hear from Erin.

'I don't want you and Dad to split up because of me. You make him happy,' Caitlin declared.

Another pause. And then Caitlin really shocked him by saying, 'Erin, you need to talk to Dad and make it up.' She handed the phone to Nate, and walked out of the room. 'Talk to her. I'm going to put the kettle on for Gran.'

Which left him no choice but to talk to her, though this was a conversation that Nate would much rather have face to face. 'Hi,' he said carefully.

'Is Caitlin OK?'

Typical Erin, thinking of someone else first. 'She is now. We've talked. We understand each other better.' He took a deep breath. 'Erin, you and I need to talk, too. But I don't want to have this conversation on the phone. My mum's coming over to sit with Cait—not because I don't trust her, but because I don't want her to be on her own.'

There was a long, long pause. And then Erin said, 'You're right. We need to have this conversation face to face.'

'Can I come over when Mum gets here?'

'OK.'

Though she sounded unsure, he thought. 'I'll see you soon.'

Once his mother and Caitlin were settled, he drove over to Erin's flat. She answered the door immediately, and he could see the strain on her face. He wanted to wrap her in his arms and keep her close, but he knew he didn't have the right to do that. Not yet. So he simply said, 'Hi. Thanks for letting me come over.'

'Coffee?'

He shook his head. 'I just need to talk to you.'

She ushered him into the living room, and to his relief she sat next to him on the sofa.

'I think maybe we need to revisit the situation,' he said, 'now I've talked to Caitlin and we understand each other. I was there when she called you, so I heard her end of the conversation—she told you you're important to both of us, and that's true.' He looked her straight in the eye. 'She's given us her blessing. You know how I feel about you, Erin, and I think you feel the same about me—even if you're too scared to say the words.'

'So you're not pulling your punches tonight, either, then?' she asked wryly.

'Erin, it's obvious you're scared. And I think you ran away tonight, just like Cait did—because you're scared to take a risk.'

'You think I'm a coward?'

'I think you're the strongest woman I know,' he said. 'But I also think you don't want to risk letting people close. It scares you. You're one of life's fixers—but you keep yourself busy and that helps you hide how vulnerable you are. From yourself, as well as from others.'

* * *

His words hit home, particularly as her brother had said the same thing. And Erin knew they were both right. She *was* scared of letting people close—scared that when they saw who she really was, she'd lose them. And she buried her fears and vulnerability beneath hard work, hiding from herself as well as others.

Could she take the risk with Nate?

As if he guessed what she was thinking, he said softly, 'Don't use Caitlin as an excuse. You know how she feels about you. You know how I feel about you. And, just so we're clear on this, I'm not looking for a mother for my daughter—I'm looking for someone for *me*. There's only one woman who's everything I'm looking for, and that's you. I know you've made mistakes in your past. They're understandable and you've more than paid for them, over the years. So when are you going to trust yourself enough to move on and have a really serious relationship—a for ever relationship?'

'But you can't want me. You don't know the full story,' she said.

'Is that another excuse to keep your protective barriers round yourself?' he asked.

It stung. Partly because she knew he was right. 'OK. You asked for this. What happened with Andrew…there were consequences.' She took a deep breath. 'He didn't use contraception and I wasn't on the Pill.'

He stared at her as if he was doing the maths in his head. 'So you have a child the same age as Caitlin?'

'No. I would've done, except I had a miscarriage,' she said. 'I'm sad that I never got to know my baby. But I'm also relieved that I didn't end up being a mum when I was too young to cope with it—and I still feel guilty about being relieved.'

'Hey. First of all, Andrew raped you. He didn't even give you a chance to say no, let alone use protection.' He wrapped his arms round her. 'Secondly, you were fifteen, so you would've been still only sixteen when the baby was born. Actually, you probably would've made a good job of being a mum, but your life would've been very different. You wouldn't have been able to train as a doctor, and I can say on your patients' behalf that that would've been a massive loss to medicine. And thirdly, it wasn't your fault that you had a miscarriage. It's one of those things that just happen. You don't have anything to feel guilty about. Anything at all.'

Could she let the guilt go, after all those years?

'Did you have anyone to support you through it?' he asked. 'You said your dad wasn't very good with emotional stuff and your mum's… well…'

'Difficult.' She nodded. 'I was in denial about being pregnant. And then, when I did face up to it, I didn't know what to do. Gill found me crying in the toilets at school and she made me talk to her mum. That's when I told Rachel about what Andrew did—and the consequences I wasn't expecting. She helped me come to terms with everything. And then, after the miscarriage, she pushed me into going back to school—a different school, one where people didn't know me and couldn't judge me, so I could re-sit my exams and get my life back together.'

'I'm sorry you had to go through such a rough

time,' he said. 'I thought I had it hard but my family was always there for me.'

'Mikey was there for me. As much as he could be.' She paused. 'So now you know the rest of it.'

'And it doesn't change my feelings for you in the slightest. Except that maybe I admire you even more. Your strength is amazing, Erin.'

'It doesn't feel that way,' she said tiredly.

He kept his arms round her. 'You're vulnerable but you've always had to be the strong one, the one who does the rescuing and sorts things out for other people.'

'And you're right when you said I used that to hide things from myself,' she said.

'Maybe,' he said, 'it's time you were the rescuee instead of the rescuer.'

'The rescuee?'

'Because what I'm going to ask you now needs a lot of strength,' he said. 'A lot of trust. You saw your parents' marriage break down—and the little you've told me makes me think that some other relationships didn't work out for them. You saw your brother's girlfriend walk away when she found out he'd be in a wheelchair. You were let down in the worst possible way by the boyfriend you thought loved you. It's understandable that you don't have a lot of trust in relationships.'

'I don't,' she admitted.

'And not being able to trust is why you've dated but it's never been really serious since,' Nate said.

She frowned. 'I thought you were a spinal surgeon, not a psychologist?'

'I am. And I'm not going to let you push me away, Erin—whether it's with a sharp remark like that or whether you walk out on me. I'm not leaving. I love you for who you are. You make my world a better place, and I want you there in the centre of my world, where you belong.'

'What does that have to do with being a rescuee?' she asked.

'What I'm asking you is hard. I'm asking you to trust that our relationship is going to make it—that it's going to be different from everything you were used to in the past. Having that kind of trust is hard to do on your own; but you don't have to be on your own any more. You've got me. And Cait. And—even though you haven't met her yet—my mum's lovely and she'll adore you.'

The way Erin's own mother didn't.

'I want to rescue you from all that loneliness and doubt, Erin. I want you to marry me. And I'm asking you to marry me because I love you and I want you to be my wife. I want you to be the centre of my family—but most of all I want you for *you*.' He took her left hand and kissed her ring finger. 'Sorry. I've timed this all wrong. I haven't got a ring to offer you, or...'

'You don't need a ring,' she said. 'Because what you're offering me is more precious than any jewellery can ever be. I love you, too, Nate. It scares me because I've never got it right in the past, and I don't want it to go wrong this time. With Caitlin, too, there's more at stake and it won't just be me who gets hurt if it goes wrong.'

'It's not going to go wrong,' Nate said. 'I believe in you. I believe in us.'

She swallowed hard. 'I do, too. And you're right—I was running away from you because I was scared I'd mess this up, the way I've messed everything up in the past. But now you've made me think about it, I realise that this time it's different. I'm not the only one trying to make things work; you're right there by my side, working with me. So I don't need excuses or barriers any more. Because I'm not alone.'

'So will you marry me, Erin?'

She leaned forward and kissed him. 'Yes.'

EPILOGUE

Six months later

'OK?' MIKEY ASKED, looking up at Erin and clearly seeing the nervousness in her eyes.

She took a deep breath. 'Yes.' And then she smiled. 'Yes. I really *am* OK, Mikey.'

'It doesn't matter that Mum decided not to come. It's probably better, actually, because you can enjoy your wedding without worrying what she's going to say to you,' Mikey said. 'And it's her problem, not yours.'

She nodded. 'Nate's mum kind of showed me that.' Sara was warm and loving, and had immediately made Erin feel as if she was part of the Townsend family. It was the first time in so many years that Erin had felt that she really belonged in a family, and the memory still brought tears to her eyes.

'Don't cry,' Mikey said hastily. 'Your make-up will run, and then Lou will kill me.'

Erin smiled. 'No, she won't. My sister-in-law loves you to bits. And so do I. That's why I asked you to walk me down the aisle.'

Mikey squeezed her hand. 'And I'm so glad that you did. I'm really proud of you, you know.'

'Thank you.' Being with Nate and Caitlin had taught her finally to accept praise gracefully. 'I'm proud of you, too.' She took a deep breath. 'Right. I'm ready to walk down that aisle and plight my troth.'

'That's my sister. Awesome as always.' He smiled back at her. 'You look beautiful.'

'Thank you.'

'And Nate's one of the good guys. Better still, he's good enough for you and he really makes you happy.'

She grinned. 'Yeah. He is and he does.'

'Then let's go get 'em, kiddo.'

The usher opened the door to the Victorian glasshouse. They'd deliberately widened the aisle to give enough room for Mikey's wheel-chair, and in front of them were rows of white wooden chairs with padded seats, with posies tied to the end chair in alternate rows and tubs of standard cream roses trained into a ball at the top of their perfectly straight stems. Light streamed through the three glass sides of the building, and the whole place felt filled with happiness.

Everyone turned round to look at Erin and Mikey as they made their way down the aisle.

At the end, Nate was waiting for her, along with Caitlin. They'd given her the choice of being Erin's bridesmaid or Nate's 'best daughter' instead of a best man, and Caitlin had loved the unconventionality of the idea. Especially as Erin had told her that she still got to have the pretty dress and could choose the colour.

And where else could they have got married but at Kew, where they'd first started to fall in love with each other and to make a family with Caitlin?

When Caitlin nudged him, Nate turned round. Erin looked amazing, wearing a simple cream knee-length shift dress; but she'd teamed it with high-heeled turquoise shoes, which matched

Caitlin's dress and Nate's tie. She carried a simple bouquet of cream roses in one hand and held Mikey's hand tightly with the other. She wasn't wearing a veil, but she'd left her hair loose, just held back from her face by a silver wire headband decorated with tiny roses, very similar to the one his daughter was wearing, too.

When she caught his eye, her face lit up with a smile that made his heart do a somersault.

And then she was standing beside him, ready to make a promise to him in front of their family and friends.

'I love you,' he mouthed.

'I love you, too,' she mouthed back.

Once the vows were made and Nate had got to do his favourite bit of the ceremony—kissing the new bride—they signed the register, posed for photographs and headed to the Orangery for the wedding breakfast. The eighteenth-century building was incredibly pretty, with its high ceilings, tall arched windows, and black-and-white-tiled floor. One end was set up for the formal wedding breakfast, with circular tables covered in white cloths and with cream rose centrepieces;

the other end was ready for the evening reception, with a small stage for the jazz trio Nate had booked flanked by massive ferns.

'I can't wait to dance with my bride,' Nate said with a grin. 'No more sneaking about in the trees in the park, with one earphone each, pretending that we're in a nightclub or what have you—tonight it's real music and a real dance-floor.'

'With trees,' she pointed out, laughing. 'We can't escape the trees. But I can't wait to dance with my new husband, either.'

After the meal, the speeches started.

Mikey tapped his glass with a knife. 'For obvious reasons, I won't be standing,' he said, 'but I'm very proud to make the speech at my sister's wedding. Thank you, everyone, for coming. My sister's a gorgeous bride, and I'm delighted to welcome Nate and Caitlin into our family. I'd like you all to raise your glasses to the bride and groom—to Erin and Nate.'

Everyone echoed the toast, and then Nate stood up. 'I'd like to thank Mikey and Lou for helping us so much with the wedding, my mum, Sara, for being generally wonderful, and Rachel and her family for coming all the way from Dundee to be with us today. Thank you all for coming to share our special day. But then, I knew we'd have a lot of people wanting to share it with us, because Erin's a very special woman and she's made a real difference to so many lives. And I'm really, really proud to call her my wife. I'd like you to raise your glasses to Erin—to my wonderful bride.'

'To Erin,' everyone chorused.

'And finally I'd like to thank my best daughter, Caitlin,' Nate said with a smile. 'Who I believe might have something to say.'

Caitlin stood up. 'Dad and Erin decided to have a best daughter instead of a best man. Long speeches can be a bit boring and my jokes are terrible, so I'm going to keep this short. All you need to know is that my dad and Erin love each other to bits, and I'm really glad they're married because they make each other really happy. And they make me happy, too,' she added. 'So please raise your glasses to my new stepmum and my dad, Erin and Nate.'

And finally it was Erin's turn to make a speech.

'I never thought I'd find the love of my life, and I definitely didn't think it would be Nate—especially when we started by having a fight over a garden,' she said with a grin. 'But we kind of worked it out—and a garden's what brought us together as a couple and as a family with Cait, so we just had to get married here. Thank you everyone for coming and sharing our special day, and I'd like you to raise a toast to my new husband and my new daughter, Nate and Caitlin.'

After the speeches, they cut the cake. And then, at last, there was the bit Nate had been waiting for.

When the jazz trio started playing a soft instrumental piece, he said to Erin, 'This is our cue,' and drew her to her feet. 'Finally I get to dance with my bride.'

As they walked into the middle of the dance floor, the pianist started to play 'Make You Feel My Love'.

'Our song,' he said softly. 'And I mean every word of it and more. I'd go to the stars, and back, for you.'

'Just as I would for you,' she said. 'I love you, Mr Townsend.'

'I love you, too, Dr Townsend,' he said.

And then, as they swayed together to the music, he kissed her.

* * * * *

If you enjoyed this story, check out these other great reads from Kate Hardy

HER PLAYBOY'S PROPOSAL
A PROMISE...TO A PROPOSAL?

BILLIONAIRE, BOSS... BRIDEGROOM?
HOLIDAY WITH THE BEST MAN
(Both in BILLIONAIRES OF LONDON *duet)*

All available now!

MILLS & BOON®
Large Print Medical

February

Seduced by the Sheikh Surgeon	Carol Marinelli
Challenging the Doctor Sheikh	Amalie Berlin
The Doctor She Always Dreamed Of	Wendy S. Marcus
The Nurse's Newborn Gift	Wendy S. Marcus
Tempting Nashville's Celebrity Doc	Amy Ruttan
Dr White's Baby Wish	Sue MacKay

March

A Daddy for Her Daughter	Tina Beckett
Reunited with His Runaway Bride	Robin Gianna
Rescued by Dr Rafe	Annie Claydon
Saved by the Single Dad	Annie Claydon
Sizzling Nights with Dr Off-Limits	Janice Lynn
Seven Nights with Her Ex	Louisa Heaton

April

Waking Up to Dr Gorgeous	Emily Forbes
Swept Away by the Seductive Stranger	Amy Andrews
One Kiss in Tokyo...	Scarlet Wilson
The Courage to Love Her Army Doc	Karin Baine
Reawakened by the Surgeon's Touch	Jennifer Taylor
Second Chance with Lord Branscombe	Joanna Neil

MILLS & BOON®
Large Print Medical

May

The Nurse's Christmas Gift	Tina Beckett
The Midwife's Pregnancy Miracle	Kate Hardy
Their First Family Christmas	Alison Roberts
The Nightshift Before Christmas	Annie O'Neil
It Started at Christmas...	Janice Lynn
Unwrapped by the Duke	Amy Ruttan

June

White Christmas for the Single Mum	Susanne Hampton
A Royal Baby for Christmas	Scarlet Wilson
Playboy on Her Christmas List	Carol Marinelli
The Army Doc's Baby Bombshell	Sue MacKay
The Doctor's Sleigh Bell Proposal	Susan Carlisle
Christmas with the Single Dad	Louisa Heaton

July

Falling for Her Wounded Hero	Marion Lennox
The Surgeon's Baby Surprise	Charlotte Hawkes
Santiago's Convenient Fiancée	Annie O'Neil
Alejandro's Sexy Secret	Amy Ruttan
The Doctor's Diamond Proposal	Annie Claydon
Weekend with the Best Man	Leah Martyn

MILLS & BOON®
Large Print – February 2017

ROMANCE

The Return of the Di Sione Wife	Caitlin Crews
Baby of His Revenge	Jennie Lucas
The Spaniard's Pregnant Bride	Maisey Yates
A Cinderella for the Greek	Julia James
Married for the Tycoon's Empire	Abby Green
Indebted to Moreno	Kate Walker
A Deal with Alejandro	Maya Blake
A Mistletoe Kiss with the Boss	Susan Meier
A Countess for Christmas	Christy McKellen
Her Festive Baby Bombshell	Jennifer Faye
The Unexpected Holiday Gift	Sophie Pembroke

HISTORICAL

Awakening the Shy Miss	Bronwyn Scott
Governess to the Sheikh	Laura Martin
An Uncommon Duke	Laurie Benson
Mistaken for a Lady	Carol Townend
Kidnapped by the Highland Rogue	Terri Brisbin

MEDICAL

Seduced by the Sheikh Surgeon	Carol Marinelli
Challenging the Doctor Sheikh	Amalie Berlin
The Doctor She Always Dreamed Of	Wendy S. Marcus
The Nurse's Newborn Gift	Wendy S. Marcus
Tempting Nashville's Celebrity Doc	Amy Ruttan
Dr White's Baby Wish	Sue MacKay

MILLS & BOON®

Why shop at millsandboon.co.uk?

Each year, thousands of romance readers find their perfect read at millsandboon.co.uk. That's because we're passionate about bringing you the very best romantic fiction. Here are some of the advantages of shopping at www.millsandboon.co.uk:

* **Get new books first**—you'll be able to buy your favourite books one month before they hit the shops

* **Get exclusive discounts**—you'll also be able to buy our specially created monthly collections, with up to 50% off the RRP

* **Find your favourite authors**—latest news, interviews and new releases for all your favourite authors and series on our website, plus ideas for what to try next

* **Join in**—once you've bought your favourite books, don't forget to register with us to rate, review and join in the discussions

Visit **www.millsandboon.co.uk**
for all this and more today!

D. C.